A Soldier of Shadows

A Shade of Vampire, Book 19

Bella Forrest

ALSO BY BELLA FORREST:

A SHADE OF VAMPIRE SERIES:

Derek & Sofia's story:

A Shade of Vampire (Book 1)
A Shade of Blood (Book 2)
A Castle of Sand (Book 3)
A Shadow of Light (Book 4)
A Blaze of Sun (Book 5)
A Gate of Night (Book 6)
A Break of Day (Book 7)

Rose & Caleb's story:

A Shade of Novak (Book 8)
A Bond of Blood (Book 9)
A Spell of Time (Book 10)
A Chase of Prey (Book 11)
A Shade of Doubt (Book 12)
A Turn of Tides (Book 13)
A Dawn of Strength (Book 14)
A Fall of Secrets (Book 15)
An End of Night (Book 16)

The Shade lives on...

A Wind of Change (Book 17)
A Trail of Echoes (Book 18)

A SHADE OF KIEV TRILOGY:

A Shade of Kiev 1
A Shade of Kiev 2
A Shade of Kiev 3

BEAUTIFUL MONSTER DUOLOGY:

Beautiful Monster 1
Beautiful Monster 2

For an updated list of Bella's books,
please visit www.bellaforrest.net

Contents

CHAPTER 1: BEN

"We know who you are, and we know what you want..."

I had no idea to whom the voice belonged, why it kept echoing in my ears, or what presence had followed River and me since leaving that Egyptian desert, but after the vision I'd just had, I knew one thing: The Oasis held answers. Answers about my past. Answers that nobody in The Shade had any clue about.

There was no doubt in my mind that the infant in

that vision had been me. I had been taken to Aviary as a newborn.

"What is it, Ben?" River asked as she stared at me. "What's wrong?"

I couldn't find my voice to explain to her what I had just seen. Not yet.

Ibrahim, who was sitting in a chair against the door of the chamber, stirred at River speaking. Opening his eyes, he looked our way. His sleepy expression turned to one of concern. "Is something wrong?"

"I need to speak to my parents," I said, swinging my legs off the narrow bed.

Ibrahim looke'd confused, but I was relieved when he just nodded. "I will go wake them." His eyes fell to River. "While I'm gone, you had better make sure that Ben doesn't lose control of himself and escape the Sanctuary."

River gulped, then nodded. "Try not to be too long," she said, her voice strained.

Ibrahim vanished from the spot, leaving River and me alone. I reached for her hand and pulled her against me, wrapping my arms around her small waist and resting my chin on her head so that I could breathe her in. Her arms slid around my midriff and she held me as we stood in silence, my mind still playing over the vision I had just experienced. The vision I had been given.

River didn't ask again what was wrong, and I was glad that she gave me space to collect my thoughts before my parents arrived five minutes later. Both were in their nightclothes as they appeared in the room alongside Ibrahim. My gut clenched on catching the strong scent of my father's blood. I backed away into the furthest corner of the room with River.

Before they could ask me what was wrong, I began to explain. "I just had a vision. I saw myself in Aviary as a newborn. Something happened to me while I was being kept there… I was carried away by a Hawk to another place briefly before being brought back again."

My father's brows furrowed. "Wait, Ben. A vision? What do you mean, a vision?"

"I mean I had a vision," I said. "Just now. As I was lying in bed with River."

"Are you sure it wasn't a dream?" my father asked.

"It wasn't a dream," I said impatiently. "I wasn't sleeping. I know that for a fact."

"What do you mean you were taken somewhere else?" my mother asked, her face tense. "Where?"

I described the place as best as I could. The black mountain ranges with their sharp peaks. The absence of greenery. The dark clouds. The sky tinged with red.

The expression on my parents' faces was one of shock.

"What?" I asked.

"Ben," my father said, "the place you've described… it sounds like Cruor."

Cruor. The land of the Elders, the original vampires.

My skin prickled as I recalled the shadowy presence that had surrounded my infant form, and that bone-chilling hiss…

"Take him back to Aviary… His time will come."

Could that have been an Elder who enveloped me? What did he mean by those words?

But none of it made any sense. "Are you sure?" I said. "How could that have been Cruor? Hawks and Elders were, and are, the deadliest of enemies. Why on earth would a Hawk take me to Cruor? Especially since my blood was supposed to be rare and valuable. Why would a Hawk risk taking me anywhere near that place?"

My parents exchanged glances. Ibrahim didn't have any insight to offer either. We just looked at each other, confused.

After moments of silence, another voice rang out in my memory. This time, it was the voice of my cousin. Jeramiah Novak.

"Something tells me you will be returning..."

After we'd first escaped from The Oasis, I'd said to River that I hoped we would never find out what he meant by those words, or why he had let her escape so easily.

Now, it appeared that I had no choice but to find out.

CHAPTER 2: RIVER

I thought that Ben had lost his mind when he said, "I need to return to The Oasis."

"What?" Ibrahim, Ben's parents and I all exclaimed at once.

"There's someone, or something, there that knows more about me than any of us do."

Sofia stepped forward and clutched her son's shoulders. "I know something about The Oasis has left its mark on you and that's why you've been having all these bizarre experiences, but this is an extremely drastic conclusion. What if all of this is just a trap to lure you back there? What if it's one of their witches creating an illusion in your head?"

"I don't doubt that it's a trap," Ben replied, "but I don't believe the vision I just had was an illusion. I don't see how they could've made that up. They know far too much about me and my past."

"But Ben," I breathed, "how can going back be the answer? Even if you did discover the truth about what happened to you and why you're like this, you could end up trapped there. There's no way of knowing whether Jeramiah would allow you to escape again. How does going back solve anything?"

To my surprise, it was Derek who replied. "I agree with Ben," he said. "And I believe him when he says that what he had was a vision, not a dream. I can't be entirely convinced that what he saw was truth, but so far, this is the closest we have come to an answer. It's the only clue we have, and I don't see how we can leave this road unexplored. So I think Ben should go back."

Apparently he was just as desperate as his son to

find an answer. Sofia gaped, turning on her husband.

"What?"

"I think Ben should return," Derek repeated calmly. He turned his eyes toward his son, who had his gaze fixed on his father. "But I don't think you should go alone. That would be foolish when we have many capable people to accompany you."

Ben looked reluctant. "I don't want to be the cause of any more casualties," he said. "This is my problem and I don't see how it's fair to expect any of our people to share my burden."

"Not expect, Ben," Derek said. "But I think that you will find that many on this island will want to help their prince."

Ben bit his lip, apparently seeing truth in his father's words.

"So far from what you've told us," Derek continued, "we know that they have an army of vampires, five witches, half-bloods and a lot of humans. Unless there was anyone else living there you didn't see, that's hardly much to contend with.

We have stood against much, much worse. You said that the witches cast a protective spell over The Oasis, but I don't see that as anything that the force of our witches combined couldn't crack. And once inside the atrium, we wouldn't leave until we'd solved this mystery—why you had that vision, why you are experiencing these voices, why you are still hearing sounds of that place even thousands of miles away."

Ibrahim cleared his throat. "Derek," he said, "before doing anything, we need to wait for Corrine. The look on her face when she was examining those tattoos... We shouldn't take her reaction lightly. She told River and Ben to wait in this room until she returned, and I really think that you should heed her advice."

Derek and Ben both let out sharp breaths. "How much longer is she going to take?" Derek asked.

Ibrahim shrugged. "You saw how she wouldn't tell any of us what she was thinking. She just said to wait."

"Well, we have waited enough," Derek said.

"Would you just go and talk to her? Even if she is not sure of whatever she suspects, she can at least give us some idea. She can't keep us in the dark any longer."

Ibrahim looked reluctant, but nodded. "I'll see what I can do."

Ibrahim vanished, leaving Derek, Sofia, Ben and me in the room.

"Of the people who are willing," Ben said, "who do you suggest we bring?"

"First off, as many witches as we can spare," Derek replied. "Then we should bring an army of vampires, werewolves… and I also suggest we bring a couple of dragons if they are agreeable."

Dragons. The notion was so strange to me. Since we had arrived, neither Ben nor I had come across any, but I had seen footage of dragons lined up along a California beach on the TV. My mother had convinced me those giant beasts had just been works of a talented CGI artist.

Ben's eyes turned on me, his hold on me tightening.

"River," he said, "I don't want any of this to affect your plans. You said that you would wait for me to turn into a human before thinking about going to visit your family. Well, now that's not possible, you need to start thinking about your own plans. I don't want to drag you any further into my problem."

My own plans... I was so overwhelmed with everything that had happened in the past twelve hours with Ben, I'd barely thought about my own plans.

As much as the idea of visiting my family thrilled me, I didn't feel comfortable about abandoning Ben. It felt like we were on this journey together, and just as he'd been there all along to help me, I ought to do the same for him. Although the idea terrified me, I found myself saying, "I want to come with you, Ben."

He immediately shook his head. "No. It's going to be far too dangerous, and I really can't see the need for you to come."

"You don't know what exactly is going to happen while you're there," I persisted, "and there might be a need for you to have my blood near you. For a start, the place is filled with humans."

"River—"

"As for danger," I continued, cutting him off, "it will be very different this time. You'll be going there with a whole army. From the way you and your father are talking, it sounds like the only ones in danger will be the residents of The Oasis themselves."

Ben looked toward his parents, as though he wanted them to back him up in convincing me to stay. Sofia set her eyes on me. And then a small smile appeared on her face.

I wasn't sure why she smiled exactly, but she said, "One thing your father and I have learned recently is to never underestimate a determined seventeen-year-old girl."

Ben looked surprised by his mother's response. He paused, then said with a sigh, "Okay. If you want to come, I won't try to stop you... But what about your family? You've been saying all this time how much they need you, how much you want to get back to them."

"I do want to visit my family," I said slowly. "But maybe I could visit them now, while you're waiting for Corrine and making preparations to leave? I would only need an hour or two." I paused, realizing that I wasn't confident in leaving Ben's side for even that amount of time.

Ben seemed to be reading my thoughts. "Yes, you could do that. And I would find a way to manage during that time."

"How will you manage? Even with me by your side, you struggle to rein yourself in."

"You won't be gone long," Ben said. "You could leave me some more of your blood, then I would go and wait in the submarine, along with perhaps four or five other vampires in case things get really bad."

He seemed to be confident in his words, so that put me at ease a little. "Okay," I said.

Ben addressed his father. "Can we spare a witch for a couple of hours? Just to transport River to New York. The plan is for her to bring her family back here to visit, if her mother agrees."

Derek nodded. "She can go with Shayla."

Ben lowered his head and pressed his lips against the side of my neck in a tender kiss. His caress sent tingles running down my spine.

"I'll manage for a couple of hours, River," he said softly. "Now, finally, go back to your family."

20257114

Chapter 3: River

Derek left the room and reappeared about ten minutes later accompanied by a witch, Shayla. She was holding a map in her hands and, after glancing in my direction, she sat down on a chair, placed the map on her knee and asked me to show her the exact location of our apartment in Manhattan.

Once she had studied it, she manifested a cup. She raised a brow at me. "Ready for me to draw some blood?"

I held out my wrist, wondering how she was going

17

to do it. Extending a forefinger, she ran it over my skin, leaving behind a thin cut. That was certainly less painful than the times I'd cut myself or Ben had dug his fangs into me. She gathered my blood into the cup.

"Shayla," Derek said, once she'd finished drawing blood, "take Ben, River and Sofia to the submarine. Sofia, you will stay with Ben there and I will find four or five other vampires to join you. You'll all wait there while River is gone."

"And you?" Sofia asked.

"I'll be gathering our army and making other preparations for leaving for The Oasis."

And so it was done. Shayla transported us to the submarine, and after I kissed Ben goodbye, he disappeared beneath the hatch with his mother. I still felt nervous about leaving him, but I repeated to myself Ben's reasoning—I wouldn't be gone long, he had a cup of my blood, and soon there would be five vampires waiting with him down there. *It's going to be okay.*

When my thoughts turned to my family, I lit up

with anticipation at the prospect of seeing them again. I could already picture the relief that would spread across my mother's face and the tears that would form in her eyes. I could hardly contain my excitement when Shayla closed her hand around my arm and our surroundings disappeared.

The ground beneath me gave way, and it felt like I was hurtling at lightning speed through an endless expanse of air. Wind whipped around me, and by the time my feet hit solid ground again, I felt dizzy.

My vision coming into focus, I found myself staring around the dark living room of our small two-bedroom apartment.

It felt so strange to be back here. Breathing in the familiar smell, feeling the carpet beneath my feet… to be home after so long, and after so many times when I'd believed that I might never see this place again.

It was early in the morning, so my family would be in their bedrooms sleeping.

Leaving the living room, I made my way through the kitchen and stopped outside my mother and Jamil's room. Pressing my ear against the door, I held my breath and listened. I could hear nothing but silence. Not even the slightest intake of breath.

When I pushed the door open, the room was empty. I hurried to the second bedroom—my, Dafne, and Lalia's room. Also empty. The bathroom door was wide open, clearly nobody inside.

Panic threatened to overtake me. I took a deep breath, trying to calm myself.

It's okay. They must all be staying with my grandfather in Cairo. I shouldn't have been surprised that after hearing of my disappearance, my mother had flown straight there. It'd make no sense that she would stay here in New York when I had been last seen near Cairo.

Still trying to fight the sick feeling in my stomach, I turned to Shayla. "I need you to transport me to Cairo," I said. "My grandfather lives there, and I know that's where my family must be."

Shayla's map only covered New York, so I started up our old computer, connected to the Internet, and pulled up a map of Cairo on the screen. After I had located the address of my grandfather, Shayla studied the map, then nodded.

"Okay," she said. "Let's go."

She touched my arm, and once again, my surroundings vanished as we traveled at lightning speed.

When we reappeared again, it was in my grandfather's backyard. We were standing by the pool. Looking toward the house, I was relieved to see that the back door was open. I wanted to rush in and start shouting out the names of my family, but I caught myself. If the hunters were still after me, this would be the logical place to keep watch. I remained holding onto Shayla's hand, just in case we had to make a speedy escape, as we entered the house.

We looked first in the small breakfast room that looked out onto the pool, then moved to the kitchen, the library, the living room, then upstairs in all the bedrooms and bathrooms. All were empty. Not even Bashira was anywhere to be found.

Now the knot in my stomach was too tight for me to even attempt to loosen.

Noticing my anguish, Shayla approached me.

"What if they're just out?"

"Why would they leave the back door open?"

"It could've just been a mistake." Heading back down the stairs, the witch pointed toward the main entrance. "Looks like they remembered to lock the front door," she said.

I walked up to it and clutched the handle. Yes, it had been locked.

"I'm going to try to call my grandfather," I said.

I picked up the handset from the coffee table in the living room and dialed my grandfather's cell number. I bit my lip as I waited.

The ringing continued until I reached voicemail.

Damn.

I could try my mother's cell phone. Though the number I knew by heart was a US SIM card. I didn't know if she would have the same one while in Cairo, and just suck up the roaming charges, or whether she would've gotten a local SIM. In any case, I tried dialing the number I knew. Voicemail again. In a last-ditch attempt, I reached for my grandfather's phonebook in the chest of drawers and paged through it until I found Bashira's number. When I dialed it, I was also unable to reach her.

Shayla was eyeing me, a look of concern on her face.

"Maybe we should wait here for a while," she said. "It could be they are in a meeting or something… They might return soon. This house doesn't feel like it's been unoccupied long."

"Okay," I said.

But I didn't want Ben to leave without me. He didn't want to take me to The Oasis in the first place, and if I had not arrived back by the time they were ready to leave, I was sure they would not wait for me.

"Let's wait for an hour, and see if my family returns," I said. I doubted Ben and the others would leave before then.

Shayla nodded and took a seat in an armchair. I was too antsy to even think about sitting down. I paced up and down the entrance hall, my heart jumping at even the slightest of noises coming from the road outside the house.

I kept looking up at the clock, watching the

minutes go by. Ever. So. Slowly.

Shayla didn't say a word to me, leaving me to brood in tense silence. After we had waited forty-five minutes, I was beginning to lose hope.

"For all we know, they could return at the end of the day," Shayla finally called from the living room. "I don't know why you're assuming that something bad—"

Her sentence was interrupted by my scream. Something had scuttled across my feet. Looking down, I was alarmed to see a huge black rat. It had gleaming yellow eyes and a creepily long gray tail. It had frozen a few feet away from me and appeared to be staring right up at me.

Backing away, I calmed my racing heart and looked toward Shayla, who had appeared in the doorway of the living room.

"It's just a rat," I said, my voice still uneven from the fright. "Just a rat," I repeated to myself as I looked back down at the creature, still frozen in the same position.

In all the times I'd stayed in my grandfather's

house, I'd never been aware that he had a rat problem. Perhaps the creature had crept in just today through the back door they had left open.

Shayla let out a soft chuckle and returned to the living room. I was about to look up once again at the clock when the rodent jolted. As if in a hurry, it scurried across the floor and, to my surprise, leapt about four feet in the air, landing on an ornamental chest of drawers by the staircase.

It turned around to face me again, its small yellow eyes looking right at me. Then something drew my attention a few inches to the right of its front feet. An object I hadn't noticed before. An object that made my heart skip a beat. I rushed forward, barely believing my eyes. When I picked up the object in my palm, it was cool, round and heavy. I was staring down at a golden coin—identical to the coins I had in my backpack. Identical to the coins that were gifted by The Oasis.

My mouth agape, I looked back toward the rat.

But it was nowhere to be seen.

Then, for the first time, I experienced the same

voice Ben had. Whispery and bone-chilling, it echoed through my head:

"Come back, River Giovanni.

"We know who you are, and we know what you want."

CHAPTER 4: CORRINE

A cool wind caught my hair as I walked among the shadowy dunes. I had known of The Oasis' location since the hunters had attacked the Maslen coven, but this was the first time that I had actually visited it. Now, of course, there was a spell concealing its entrance. This would make it harder for me to detect it… but I did not need its exact location.

Once I sensed that I had neared within a hundred feet of its boundary, I stopped. Parting my cloak, I unhitched the long wooden staff that I had attached to my belt, along with a brass container of potion I'd prepared in my kitchen and a clear glass cup. I set the last two items down on the sand while I eyed the length of the staff. Positioning the pointed end of it above the ground, I dug it into the sand, pushing it down until it felt secure in its upright position. I picked up the glass cup and, with my magic, made it balance atop the tip of the staff. Then I reached for the brass container and emptied its dark blue contents into the glass.

I watched the potion settle into the cup, watching as it began to stiffen. I had expected to need to manifest some light to see what I was doing, but the sky was clear and the moon was full tonight.

I looked down at my watch and noted the time. *Now I must wait.*

My mind wandered back to the tattoos I'd seen on River and Ben's upper arms. Even as I thought of them, the same fear gripped me. I hadn't wanted to speak a word of my suspicion to anyone, not even Ibrahim, until I was certain. So I'd headed straight back to the Sanctuary, locked myself in my library, and pulled down all the books on the subject that I could find. It had become clear to me after half an hour of paging through the dusty manuscripts that the only way for me to know for certain if my fear was founded was to come out here and see if I could detect the presence of these creatures myself.

Jinn.

I had never had direct experience with their kind, but I had read about them in the texts of my ancestors. And what I had read about them was enough to leave me terrified.

Even among supernaturals, they were creatures of legend. Many believed them to be fairy tales made up by humans, since they were so rarely spotted. I wasn't aware of anyone who knew where they resided back in the supernatural realm.

My mind was pulled back to the present moment as a sudden movement on the sand about ten feet away from me caught my attention. Something round was moving directly toward me, so fast that I had to strain my eyes to see what it was.

A huge beetle. Its sturdy body was covered in a

dark-green shell that glinted eerily beneath the moonlight. I wasn't sure why it was scuttling toward me. Perhaps it fancied me as food—it certainly looked big and sturdy enough to take a bite out of me.

I wasn't fond of beetles. Nor any insect for that matter. Not willing to wait around to see what this beetle's agenda was, I zapped it with a spell that sent it hurtling through the air and landing somewhere far in the distance.

Shuddering, I focused my attention back on the potion. It was still the same dark blue color, but it had become completely solid. Now I just had to wait for it to change color. I looked down at my watch. I should have my answer in five minutes, and then I could leave this place and return to the safety of The Shade... I prayed I'd return with better news than I'd come here expecting.

Only two minutes had passed when my attention was again drawn in the same direction the beetle had approached me from. This time, I laid eyes on not an insect, but a long, beige-colored snake. A horned rattlesnake, by the looks of it. As it approached me in exactly the same manner as the beetle had, a chilling suspicion dawned on me.

I need to get out of here. Now.

As much as it pained me to abandon my experiment that I'd gone to such effort to prepare, this coincidence of the snake and the beetle had spooked me too much to remain. I yanked the staff from the ground and, discarding the glass of stiff potion, I vanished from the spot… At least, I tried to vanish. Summoning my powers, I closed my eyes, expecting to feel the wind whipping past me as I began hurtling back toward the island. But the sand remained beneath my feet. No matter how hard I tried to vanish, I didn't budge.

I opened my eyes to see the snake now only six feet away from me. It had stopped, and I could have sworn that its small, narrow eyes were fixed directly on me. Then its body began to contract. Its beige scales darkened until they'd turned an almost pitch black. Its head and tail shrank in toward the middle of its body until it had formed a fleshy ball. The ball began to spin in its place until four feet shot out from it. Then a head. A long tail. A few seconds later, I was staring down at an oversized black rat.

But the vision remained before me for barely ten seconds before again, the creature's limbs withdrew into itself, forming another ball and this time re-manifesting as a red scorpion. Then a jackal. Then a vulture… until finally, all the terror I'd felt on first seeing those tattoos cemented itself in my mind as I stood staring into the piercing golden eyes of a creature rarely spoken of, much less seen.

Then a silvery voice spoke in my head:

"Is your curiosity now satisfied, witch of The Shade?"

Horror welled in the pit of my stomach.

I'd just been granted a wish by a jinni.

Chapter 5: Ben

Imagining River reuniting with her family warmed me. I'd seen how much family meant to her, how close she was to her mother and siblings. I'd seen the pain in her eyes every time she had spoken of them. Now she would finally see them again, and if all went to plan, Shayla would return with them to The Shade within about an hour.

After River left, I kept the cup of her blood close to me as my mother sat by my side in the submarine. I still hadn't expressed what I felt about River to my parents, or even Rose, but I hadn't exactly kept my affection for her secret.

My mother tried to make some small talk as we sat together, but her mind was clearly weighed down by the worry of my failed turning. Though she didn't speak of it, I could see it behind her eyes.

Caleb, Rose, my grandfather and Griffin arrived through the hatch soon after River had left. This was the first time that I had seen my grandfather since arriving back. He moved toward me and gripped me in a tight hug.

"You don't know how relieved I am to see you again, Ben," he said, kissing the top of my head.

"I'm glad to be back," I said. *I just wish I could stay.*

I was surprised to see that Griffin was a vampire. Grinning, he held up his hands in mock reproach. "Come on. What chance did a human ginger boy stand on an island of vampires and dragon shifters?"

I smirked, then drew him in for a hug and slapped him on the back.

"You look great," I said, giving him a wink which made my sister giggle.

My sister turned to me. It was still bizarre to see my twin as a vampire. I wasn't sure how long it would take me to get used to it, if I ever would. I guessed that she'd be feeling the same about me.

She stood on her tiptoes and kissed my cheek.

"How are you feeling?" I asked.

She grimaced. "Hungry. Thirsty. Can't really decide which it is. I just want to raid a blood bank."

I know the feeling.

I was glad that she was sensitive enough to not ask how I was feeling. It was obvious how I was feeling after what had just happened.

"Dad sent us," she said, changing the subject. "He told us to wait with you for the next hour or so, until he's finished organizing the army and planning the trip. Obviously, I'll be coming, and Caleb will too."

We moved to the control room where there was more seating.

Rose and Griffin began to share some banter while I looked out toward the dark island. *The Shade. Will it ever be my home again the way it once was? Will I ever be able to roam its beautiful beaches and forests again without being a constant threat to our human residents?*

The island looked so peaceful at this early hour. The redwood trees swayed gently in the wind, the glistening ocean waves lapping against the shore.

Having lived here since I was five, I had taken this place for granted. It was only now that I couldn't have it that I realized just how much I appreciated my home.

I caught sight of Shadow in the distance, racing full speed along the beach. Eli was about half a mile behind him, walking alone. I smiled as the dog raced toward the waves and began splashing about as he chased his tail. That dog had the spirit of a puppy with the strength of a rhino. But if it weren't for him, I didn't know if I would've even seen the light of day—my mother might've never escaped the Elder's grasp.

I continued watching the dog from my seat, but then stood up as a screeching pierced the quiet morning. Shadow's strong jaws had clamped around something.

"A mermaid," my mother gasped. "He's caught that mermaid."

We all watched in horror as he dragged the creature onto the sand. His jaws were clamped around her left arm. If he let go and bit into another part of her body, there was no way she'd survive the attack.

Having noticed what had happened, Eli sped up along the beach. He shouted something at the dog, a word I couldn't recognize, and Shadow instantly let go of the mermaid. As she squirmed across the sand back into the waves, she left a trail of blood behind.

My father had said that he would ask Ibrahim to get rid of these creatures from our waters, but it appeared that they had both been too preoccupied to see to this yet.

By some strange coincidence, almost as soon as I thought of the warlock, he appeared before us in the center of the control room. There was a sheen of sweat on his brow and his face looked strained.

"I can't find Corrine," he said, looking around the room at each of us before his eyes settled on me and my mother.

"What do you mean you can't find her?" my mother asked.

"She's not in the Sanctuary. I gathered together a search party of other witches, vampires and werewolves. We've searched every nook and cranny of The Shade looking for her. I even visited the dragons' mountain quarters to see if she might have gone there for some reason. None of the fire-breathers had seen her. She must've left the island."

I frowned. "For what?"

"Your guess is as good as mine," he said.

"And we have no idea when she'll be back," my mother said, her expression mirroring Ibrahim's. "That means that unless she returns within the next one to two hours, we're going to have to leave without her. Derek isn't going to want to hang around."

Ibrahim looked anything but happy with the idea, but he nodded. "I hope that she'll return before then."

I was just pondering over where the witch might've

gone when more people appeared in the room. River and Shayla. I was surprised to see only the two of them. I'd been expecting River's family to arrive. From the look on their faces, it was clear that something had gone seriously wrong.

River looked at me with panic in her eyes.

"The Oasis. They've taken my family."

CHAPTER 6: DEREK

Thoughts of the hunters surrounding our island slipped from my mind for the first time in weeks as I went about making preparations to leave for The Oasis.

I was just making my way around the vampires' residences, gathering up those who were willing to come, when Sofia came rushing toward me. I was surprised to see her away from our son.

"What's wrong?" I asked as she reached me. I feared for a moment Ben had gone berserk again and done something horrifying.

"River and Shayla returned. They went to her apartment in New York, and they also went to Cairo. River couldn't find her family and she's convinced that The Oasis has taken them. Also, Ibrahim can't find Corrine. Did he tell you?"

Sofia was speaking so fast, I was still processing the first piece of news. "I haven't bumped into the warlock since we parted ways earlier. What makes River so certain that The Oasis has her family?" I asked, frowning.

"She saw something strange in her grandfather's house in Cairo. A rat that appeared to be under some kind of supernatural influence. It left behind a gold coin—identical to those she had been given in The Oasis. She's extremely shaken by it."

"And Corrine? Has Ibrahim searched everywhere on the island?"

"He says so."

Where has that witch gone? I had no idea what had gotten into her head, but we couldn't hold things up for her any longer. She couldn't expect us to wait for her indefinitely when she hadn't given us even the faintest idea of what we were waiting for. As much as I respected Corrine, sometimes her way of doing things irritated the hell out of me.

I drew in a deep breath. "Okay. You should go back and wait in the sub with Ben. Tell River that we will leave as soon as possible."

Sofia nodded, then hurried off.

Now we have a second reason to storm the place.

So far, I had gathered Xavier, Ashley, Landis, Gavin, Zinnia, Matteo, Helina, Erik, and three dozen other vampire guards. Yuri hadn't yet turned back into a vampire, and so was off limits. Liana and Cameron were also still human—and besides, they were still finding their feet after a long journey. And, of course, Claudia and Vivienne were pregnant.

I had told those who'd volunteered to go and wait by the Port. Now I was on my way to see Mona and Kiev, and then our werewolf residents. I continued rushing through the forest and stopped beneath the couple's tree. When I reached the top of the elevator, the lights in their penthouse were all off.

I knocked on the door. Mona answered a minute later. Her hair was scrunched up above her head in a messy bun and she was wearing a bathrobe.

"Derek?"

"We're gathering an army to storm The Oasis."

Kiev appeared behind Mona in the shadowy doorway, his hair ruffled. Wearing a dark green robe, he also looked like he had just gotten out of bed.

"When?" he asked.

I was surprised by Kiev's question. I'd expected him to first ask "why". But I couldn't help but feel grateful to the vampire for being so willing to stand by our side in times of need. As much as I'd loathed having to admit or even believe it at first, Kiev truly was part of our family.

"As soon as I've finished gathering our army together," I replied. "But if you want to come, I'd like you to go and wait by the Port now."

Kiev looked down at his wife. "Will you come?"

She shrugged, glancing at me. "You know I'm still working on building up my powers again, and I'm not nearly as powerful as the other witches on this island anymore. But if Kiev's going… yeah, I'll come too. We'll get dressed and head to the Port."

"Thank you," I said.

They closed the door and I made my way back down the elevator to move toward my next stop. The residences of the werewolves. Many had decided to remain living in the houses we had designated for them along one of the beaches, while others had moved into mountain cabins.

When I arrived at the beach, the first door I knocked on was Saira's. Since the sun hadn't risen yet, she was still in her wolf form as she answered. I explained to her the purpose of my visit, and she was more than willing to accompany us. She also agreed to rally as many other werewolves as she could and bring them to the jetty as soon as possible. She would also speak to the wolves who lived in the mountain cabins, which left me free to set all my attention on my last stop—the dragons' quarters within the Black Heights.

As I made my way toward the mountains, the thought of coming face to face with Jeramiah—a nephew we hadn't even known existed just days ago—played on my mind. I wondered how much he would resemble my brother. Ben hadn't been able to quite put a finger on his personality. While the vampire's demeanor seemed calm and amenable, there was clearly a lot more to him than met the eye.

I regretted never being able to have a normal relationship with my brother. A relationship that involved anything other than hatred. And I couldn't deny that the last thing I wanted to do was harm my dead brother's son. Jeramiah was my own blood. After I'd gathered the army, I would make it clear to everyone that we weren't going to The Oasis to kill or harm anyone, just to get the answers we needed about Ben, and retrieve River's family—if indeed they had been taken there.

The truth was, if I saw any way to make peace with my nephew, I would take it. I would do everything I could to avoid violence and come to some kind of understanding. I didn't know how much he knew of his past. Since no one from The Shade had ever heard of or been aware of him, he truly must've lived a life away from the rest of the vampire world. Ben had said that his mother had died when he was just a child, and much of his life he had spent alone, or as a captive of the Elders in their Himalayan coven. I hadn't even been aware that a coven existed in India. It just showed the reach of the Elders when they'd been at the peak of their hold on this realm.

Ben also didn't seem to think that Jeramiah had recognized him. Since I resembled Lucas quite closely, and Benjamin resembled me, I was surprised that Jeramiah hadn't noticed similarities between Ben and himself. Or at least Ben and Lucas. But then, I doubted that Jeramiah had even seen a photograph of his father, since I was sure that Lucas and Jeramiah's mother hadn't had a relationship other than a few stolen meetings in the mill near our farm.

Whatever the case, and however much he might know about us, I was determined to keep my cool with the young man as long as possible.

Arriving at the foothills of the Black Heights, I pushed aside thoughts of my newfound nephew and walked through the entrance leading to the dragons' quarters.

I passed through the stately entrance hall, dimly lit with candles, and made my way along the winding corridors. The place was so quiet at this early hour, the most I could hear was my own breathing.

Considering how much time the dragons had been on this island, I hadn't had much interaction with them. Not that it bothered me. As long as they behaved themselves—did right by the human girls they were courting and obeyed the rules of the island—I didn't mind. Their reclusiveness meant less for me to deal with.

I stopped outside Jeriad's door. I wasn't sure if he would be awake yet, but I knocked all the same.

A faint moan came from within the apartment, that of a female. There were soft footsteps, and then the door opened. An intoxicating scent of burning incense wafted out and I found myself staring down at Sylvia, one of my daughter's classmates. And the girl that Jeriad had chosen for himself.

Sylvia looked flustered. She wore a satin-gray nightgown that had clearly been put on in a hurry.

Her cheeks were bright pink, and her lips swollen and red. Her blonde hair was disheveled, but even as she looked at me, she could barely keep a grin off her face.

"Oh, hi, Mr. Novak," she said breathlessly.

Then the dragon himself appeared behind her, naked from the waist up.

To my surprise, he didn't even look in my direction. His eyes were fixed on Sylvia. Approaching her from behind, he slid a palm over the front of her neck and gently bent her head back until it touched his chest. He dipped down and kissed her full on the mouth. His tan form was so imposing, his hands so broad as he settled them either side of her hips, it looked like he could crush her midriff into a pulp with a slight squeeze.

Well, it certainly doesn't look like I've woken anyone up...

After lifting his mouth from hers several moments later, finally, he looked up to see who had knocked on his door. His blue eyes were hooded and misty as he met my gaze.

I cleared my throat.

"King Derek," he said, his voice smoky.

"Jeriad," I said, unamused by the wait. "Would you be willing, along with two of your comrades, to make a journey to Egypt?"

He paused. "Egypt?"

I'd forgotten that I was talking to a creature who'd only recently arrived in this human realm. He wasn't familiar with Earth's countries. The only place he'd visited was The Shade.

"Egypt is a country… But more specifically, our destination is a place called The Oasis. I'm not sure if you're aware of the problems my son has been having."

"My love mentioned his troubles briefly." He ran a hand over Sylvia's stomach. "It's because he was born to be a fire wielder, is it not?"

I heaved a sigh. "That may or may not be the case… We tried to turn him back into a human, when he might've developed fire powers just like my daughter. But now there's no choice to turn back. The turning failed and he's stuck as a vampire. We're trying to figure out how and why this is. And we believe The Oasis holds answers."

"What exactly do you need us for?" the shifter asked. "You want to scorch the place?"

"No," I said firmly. "We do not want to scorch the place. At least, that is not my plan. The problem is, we don't know exactly what we will find there. We know that The Oasis is home to witches and vampires, but I'm hoping that we won't need you for anything. It's just in case something goes wrong and we are in need of extra force that I would like three of you to accompany us."

He moved his head down toward Sylvia again and caressed her cheek with his mouth, turning it three shades pinker, if that was even possible. Then he raised his eyes back to me.

"I'm willing to help," he said, "and I'm sure two of my fellow dragons will be agreeable also. But when would we leave?"

"Now. I need you at the Port."

A flicker of disappointment played across Sylvia's face, as her hands tightened around Jeriad's wrists.

The dragon too looked irritated at the thought of leaving her, but he nodded. "Very well."

I stepped away and turned around, the sound of the door shutting behind me.

Hopefully, it would be no more than fifteen minutes before the dragons showed up. And by now, if all had gone according to plan, the rest of our army would be waiting for me. Except the witches... I was counting on Ibrahim to gather them together.

I made my way swiftly to the Port. I was glad to see Ibrahim already there along with all the witches, werewolves, and vampires. Approaching the warlock, I asked, "Has Corrine still not been found?"

He shook his head, his forehead wrinkled with worry.

There wasn't a lot more to be said on that subject. We weren't going to wait for her, so we could only hope that she would show up in the meantime and be here when we returned.

Three dragons appeared in the sky only seven minutes later. Their heavy wings beat forcefully, causing the trees to sway to and fro. They touched down in the clearing before the Port, their weight sending tremors through the ground.

Taking in the army, now complete, I couldn't help but feel that it was excessive. Because despite Corrine's reaction, based on what Ben and River had seen of The Oasis during their stay, I was still hoping that compared to other expeditions we had been on in the past, this one would be fairly simple...

CHAPTER 7: BEN

I did what I could to comfort River after she told me what had happened. I gathered her in my arms and held her close, trying to think of something I could say to reassure her.

I was surprised that she didn't cry. Although she looked close to it, she held back the tears. Her family was everything to her. For her to remain composed at a time like this showed a deeper strength to River than I had previously imagined.

I brushed my lips against her forehead as I held her

in my arms. "We'll find your family," I said. "Just like we saved your sister before, we'll figure out a way to save all of them this time."

"Hopefully it will be easier this time than last," she said, swallowing hard, "since we will have so much help from The Shade's residents."

I nodded, hoping that it would indeed be easy. I felt like I was at the end of my tether. Not being able to turn back into a human was the final straw for me. I just wanted to be normal, and I would do anything to make myself that again. To regain my life. My sanity.

"It's time," Caleb called down from the top of the hatch. He had been watching the beach for my father's signal.

Griffin, Rose, my grandfather, my mother, River and I left the control room, and climbed up through the hatch onto the roof of the submarine.

I looked toward the beach, where a large gathering had formed. My eyes were immediately drawn to the dragons, as were River's. Our breaths hitched. Covered in a thick armor of gleaming scales and equipped with huge leathery wings and a sting-like tail, they were spectacular creatures I'd truly believed existed only in fairytales.

One of the witches, Leyni, appeared on the roof of our submarine, and she transported all of us by magic to the jetty. I looked around at all those who'd gathered, making eye contact with all the familiar faces, many of whom I still had not seen since I'd left the island.

Micah was the first to approach me, nuzzling my leg with his head. Others greeted me also in the short time we had before my father spoke up.

He was looking toward the dragons. "Since Jeriad, Neros and Ridan refuse to be transported anywhere by magic, one of us is going to have to fly with them to make sure that they arrive at The Oasis." He looked toward my grandfather. "I was thinking you, Aiden. Do you remember its location from all those years ago when your hunters stormed the place?"

My grandfather paused. "Approximately. Obviously, I'll need a—"

Eli stepped forward, handing Aiden some kind of

flashing box-shaped device. "This will help you navigate there easily. I've already entered the coordinates."

"How long will it take you to get there?" I asked. I had absolutely no idea of the speed at which dragons could fly.

Aiden shrugged. "I'm not sure exactly. Although it's obviously not as fast as by magic, which is practically instantaneous, dragons do still travel at supernatural speed… It should be within hours. Since your father is planning not to use them anyway, it doesn't matter if we get there a bit later."

"I'll go with you," a werewolf near Aiden growled.

"Are you sure, Kailyn?" Aidan asked, looking down at her and raising his brow. "It's not going to be a comfortable ride."

"I'm sure. I'll come."

Kailyn. I guessed that was my grandfather's new girlfriend.

"All right," my father said, impatience in his voice. "Let's go."

Ibrahim cast a spell of shadow over Aiden to

protect him from the sun during the journey, before Aiden and Kailyn sped toward one of the dragons. The beast lowered his massive hands, helping the couple climb up onto his back. Then the three dragons spread their mighty wings and launched upward, beating up a gale-force wind all around us.

Once they were in the air, the rest of us formed a large circle in the clearing, making sure each of us were touching. Then my father gave the signal, and the witches made us all vanish.

CHAPTER 8: BEN

When the wind stopped howling around me and I opened my eyes, it was the strangest feeling to find myself standing back in the same desert I'd fought for so many weeks to escape.

By now, the sun had almost peeked above the horizon. We needed to move fast, or the witches would need to put a shield over us vampires to protect us from the rays.

Looking around the area, I spotted the hunters' tanks in the distance. There were several more of them now than there had been before, apparently still waiting and watching this area for supernaturals coming in and out of The Oasis.

I looked at Ibrahim. "You should put a protective spell over all of us now, even if it won't take long to get inside." I nodded toward the direction of the tanks. "Don't underestimate these hunters." Ibrahim nodded grimly.

While he, Mona and two other witches put up protection over all of us, I caught my father looking toward the hunters. He had a mild look of irritation on his face. A strong gust of wind passed through our crowd, bringing his scent closer to me. Although I was already standing next to River, I pulled her even closer to me and backed away from my father.

After the spell had been cast, I moved with River to the front of the crowd and we began walking closer to where I remembered the boundary had been. We led everyone forward for perhaps five minutes. My hands held out in front of me, I kept expecting to collide with the boundary. But after ten minutes, we were still walking through the expanse of desert.

We'd come far past where the boundary should have been—that much was clear to both River and me.

River looked up at me, a look of confusion on her face.

"Where is it?" she breathed.

I had no answer.

I turned to look at our companions, their eyes all fixed on us expectantly.

"We should have reached the boundary by now," was all I could say. "This... this makes no sense." I looked around, seeing nothing but endless dunes of sand.

"Are you sure this is the right direction?" my mother asked. "Is there no way you could have been mistaken?"

I was sure that this was the spot, but I was so bewildered as to why we had not already reached it that I scanned our surroundings again all the same.

I shook my head. "No. River and I have just led you right up to it—heck, through it. We should be standing above the atrium right now..."

"Is it possible that they got rid of the boundary?"

The question came from Kiev.

"Why on earth would they do that?" I said. "And even if they had gotten rid of it, there should be a camel stable in view. Plus an entrance in the ground… It's almost like it's just vanished from the face of the earth."

"That's impossible," River said beneath her breath. "We've got to have been mistaken about the spot, Ben."

"Then where do you think it is?" I said, turning on her.

She looked clueless as she eyed the area. It was clear that she had no other suggestion either.

No. This was the spot. I remembered the area too well. Besides, there were the hunter tanks stationed nearby.

I kept walking forward, even though I didn't know what the use was. I just didn't know what else to do. Admit defeat and return to The Shade? I was partly in shock. This bizarre turn of events was still sinking in when someone yelled out a curse behind me.

It was Ashley. Sitting down on the ground, she was

cradling her right foot. A slew of four-letter words continued to flow from her lips as I hurried over to her along with Landis and several others. Blood was seeping from her foot and staining the sand.

"What happened?" Landis asked, alarmed.

"Argh," was all the reply he got from her as she removed her shoe and sock to reveal a deep slice through the sole of her foot. Although it was clearly causing her agony, at least, as a vampire, she would heal quickly. The corners of the gash had already started to close up before our eyes.

"How did you do that?" Rose asked, planting a hand on Ashley's shoulder and squatting down next to her.

"I stepped on like a… freaking samurai sword," Ashley panted, wincing and biting her lip.

I was already examining the ground nearby, following the trail of blood.

It definitely wasn't a samurai sword. But what it was made my heart pound. A long wide dent in the ground.

Rushing over to it, River and I brushed away a thin

layer of sand to reveal the metal door leading down into the atrium. Ashley's foot had smacked into one of its sharp corners.

Relief and yet more confusion filled my mind.

"But if this is here," she said, "then where is the camel—?"

The two of us had already spotted it before she finished her question. Standing perhaps a hundred feet from us was the camel stable. Just a few seconds before when I'd looked around along with everyone else, it had been nowhere in sight.

What is going on?

As if in answer to the question, my tattoo began to tingle again, and the whispery voice echoed through my head:

"Welcome back, Benjamin Novak."

The blood drained from River's face, her lips parting. She locked eyes with me. "Did you hear that?"

I nodded.

"We are inside now?" Micah said, looking around, dumbstruck.

My mind was already racing with the implications of what had just happened. Leaving Ashley, whom Landis was helping to stand up, I darted forward. I was in such a hurry, I didn't even grab River's hand to keep her close to me. I just raced forward, desperate to reach the boundary. This time, I did find it. My outstretched hands touched the invisible hard surface. I staggered back.

The boundary. Nowhere to be found on our way in. Up like a brick wall when trying to get out.

A wave of déjà vu washed over me as I recalled the first time I'd realized I was shut in here. Now, it was all of us.

CHAPTER 9: RIVER

I could neither understand nor believe it. *What just happened?* It was as though all signs of the boundary had disappeared just to lure all of us inside, and then it had shot up again, like a Venus flytrap.

"So," Derek said, his jaw tense. "We're inside."

Ben pointed to the trapdoor. "And that is the entrance to the atrium."

The crowd gathered around, eyeing the metal door.

"This place is so different to how I remember it,"

Derek said. "All of this above here, it used to be an actual oasis—a basin of water, trees, now it's just... sand."

"Well, when the hunters attacked all those years ago, they blew the entire roof off the place," Sofia said. "They decimated the whole area. Perhaps it's never been the same since."

"Whatever the case," Ibrahim said, "before we venture any further, I want to test the strength of the boundary."

He and Mona gathered together their fellow witches and then they vanished, reappearing close to the barrier. We watched in silence as they huddled close to each other, and all at once raised their palms—releasing a spell, I assumed.

A blinding flash of light seared my eyes, forcing me to close them. And then came the deafening sound of an explosion.

A powerful force blasted toward me and I found myself thrown backward, landing on the ground. It was as though a bomb had just gone off. I tried to open my eyes when I sensed the light had softened, but particles of sand flew everywhere. I was forced to keep them closed until it settled. Then, when I looked around, it was to see that almost everyone else except for a few vampires, including Ben, had also taken shelter on the ground.

I'd never seen this spell being performed before, so I had no idea whether this kind of reaction was to be expected. But from the looks on everyone's faces, it appeared not. When my eyes traveled toward the witches, they were nowhere in sight.

"Mona!" Kiev bellowed.

Our crowd raced toward where the group of witches had been standing, the ground now scorched... and empty. Vampires and werewolves looked around frantically, while I headed straight for the boundary with Ben.

My outstretched hands were forced into balls as they brushed up against the barrier—solid as ever.

Everyone was lost for words as they continued looking hopelessly for the witches. There weren't even any bodies lying around.

Vampires and werewolves began taking turns in

testing the boundary—only to be forced back just as Ben and I had been.

"Where the hell did they go?" Kiev said, panting.

As speculations abounded among our crowd, my and Ben's eyes lowered to the ground. We seemed to be sharing the same suspicion.

"Whatever that explosion was," Ben spoke up, "I doubt the witches are dead. It doesn't seem to have been meant to kill them. Otherwise where are their bodies?"

"What are you thinking?" Sofia asked.

"I can't shake the feeling they've been taken down into The Oasis," he said.

Maybe they're down there with my family. I hated to think where they might be keeping them. I guessed the most likely place was those prisons again.

"Well, we can't get out," Derek said. "That much I think we can all agree on. We have no choice but to go down."

"Perhaps the witches here hold more power than we estimated," Sofia said. "These residents of The Oasis, they must have sensed our presence in the desert and allowed us to enter the boundary. I guess they also sensed we had our own witches and wanted to take them out…"

"Let's go down," Kiev said impatiently, running toward the trapdoor.

Ben caught my hand and pulled me after him.

"Vampires and werewolves, that's all we have now," I said to Ben as we ran. "And even when those dragons arrive with your grandfather, it's not like they could even get in through the boundary. Our witches couldn't. I can't see how the dragons could. Are we left with enough force to stand against The Oasis?"

"I don't know," Ben said heavily. "But now we've no choice but to keep moving."

He bent down and along with Kiev, his father, and Xavier, heaved at the trapdoor and forced it open.

A chill formed at the back of my neck and crept down my spine as I found myself looking down at the familiar sight of the atrium. It felt like everyone was holding their breath as we listened for any signs of life from within.

My own ears could pick up nothing but the sounds that had been echoing in my head the past weeks ever since I left. The sounds of The Oasis had previously been in my mind, now I was experiencing them live again. Except the grinding of the machine... I couldn't hear that right now.

Derek and Kiev were about to begin descending the staircase when Ben stopped them. "Wait. I want to go down first."

Ben didn't wait for the men's response. After I had slid onto his back, he pushed through the crowd and moved down the steps with me. Then he paused, looking up toward his father, who was about to follow after us with Kiev. Ben shook his head. "No, don't come yet. Wait until I say."

I sensed the guilt in Ben's demeanor. He hadn't wanted anyone accompanying him here to begin with, and now that things had gone so wrong and we had lost our witches, he was feeling the weight of responsibility.

Kiev looked like he was about to ignore Ben's request and come down anyway, but Derek gripped his shoulder and held him back. "We'll do as Ben says," he said. "But we won't wait more than five minutes." Derek shot a stern look at his son. "Come back by then, or we'll come down."

Ben nodded curtly, then continued down the staircase with me. The familiar scent of jasmine drifting up from the gardens below filled my nostrils. Arriving on the topmost platform of the atrium, Ben and I paused, looking down and taking in The Oasis' sinister beauty.

Ben's grip around my calves tightened. Despite the fear clawing at my chest, his hold on me brought me a sense of reassurance I hadn't thought possible in this terrifying place.

Chapter 10: Ben

I wasn't sure exactly what I was going to do now that I was down here with River alone, with my family and everyone else waiting up in the desert, but after what had just happened, I wanted to be the first down here to see what the situation was.

When I looked around, there wasn't a person in sight. Even as I listened, I could barely make out a sound. But this shouldn't have been surprising. The Oasis was known to be quiet in the morning, because its residents had a habit of staying up late into the night. The familiar quiet noises of the atrium filled my ears—the distant dripping of a tap, the occasional splashing of fish in the ponds, the whistling of the draught from the desert above.

After observing the upper layers of the atrium for a minute, I entered the elevator with River and we made our way down to deeper levels.

River's soft mouth brushed against my left ear. "Where do you think everyone is?" she breathed.

"I guess asleep," I said.

Though clearly somebody was awake. And that somebody was the person we needed to seek out. The person responsible for taking our witches and causing the boundary to clamp down on us.

We traveled down several floors and stopped halfway down.

"So what now?" River whispered. "We only have a few more minutes before they come down."

I didn't answer, and instead kept moving swiftly but silently around the verandas. Then, reentering the elevator, we moved down to the ground level, which appeared to be as empty as the others. Once I was satisfied that there appeared to be no immediate threat, I didn't see another option but to return to the others. Kiev had been chomping at the bit when I'd left him, he wouldn't be held up much longer.

As I motioned to retreat, River suggested, "You could send me back, and you could stay down here to keep watch?"

"No," I whispered back. "I don't want you separated from me."

We took the elevator together back up to the top level, where I hurried up the staircase. Reaching the top, I poked my head out.

River gasped.

And I instantly felt like a fool for not guessing this might happen.

There wasn't a single person in sight.

It felt like someone had just driven a knife through my chest. As if the guilt wasn't already hard enough for me to bear…

Shock soon turned to anger.

River insisted that I check the camel stables just in case, and I did, but of course, they were filled with nothing but camels.

No. Something, someone, in this place was messing with us.

"We'll go back down," I said, trying to steady my breathing. I raced across the sand and reentered the trapdoor with River. My hands closed even more tightly around her calves. She was the only person I had left, and I sure as hell was not going to lose her. They'd have to pry her from my dead hands.

Arriving back on the topmost level, I was about to rush toward the elevator when River said, "Look!"

She was pointing to my right. I turned my head to see a large leopard with a rich silky coat, standing perfectly upright. His forelegs were tucked neatly in front of him as he watched us through orange eyes.

"A leopard?" River whispered.

I nodded slowly, maintaining eye contact with the creature. I wondered what he wanted. When he hadn't budged after ten seconds, I grew tired of waiting and continued toward the elevator. But as soon as I made to move, the leopard let out a low purr and moved from his spot. Bolting across the floor with alarming speed, he planted himself directly in front of me, blocking the entrance to the elevator. Irritated by the distraction, I was about to force him aside. But then the elevator doors slid open and he stepped right in, making room for me. I followed him in, keeping a close eye on him as we descended in case he took a liking to River's flesh.

Pushing aside thoughts of this animal, I tried to organize my panicking mind. I had to be calm and collect my thoughts, or there would be no hope for any of us.

I decided that my first stop should be Lloyd's apartment. Despite the way we had parted, he always had been friendly to me, and besides, he seemed to be the weak type—possibly the easiest to scare and get information out of. I hit the button for his level—the same level my apartment had been on.

To my aggravation, although I'd hit the button twice to make sure it registered, the elevator continued descending right past the level.

This had never happened before in all the time I'd spent here. That it should happen when I was in the worst of hurries was just my luck…

I tried to stop us on the next floor down, but the elevator didn't stop there either. I kept pushing the buttons for each of the levels we passed by, but the elevator doors remained tightly shut. We were forced to remain inside until we reached the lowest level, when finally the doors slid open. The leopard sprang from his spot in the corner and padded outside before me. Not bothering to see if the second elevator that ran parallel to this one would be working, I hurried out toward the gardens, intending to just leap up to Lloyd's level.

"Brace yourself," I muttered to River, as her arms tightened around me.

Another purr came from behind me—much louder than the last, it bordered on a growl. I looked back to see that the leopard had followed us. He sat in that same neat position only five feet away.

I was about to ignore him again when he did something with his head that arrested my attention. He moved it sharply to the right, toward the opposite side of the atrium. I could have sworn that he was nodding. Then he began moving toward the direction he'd indicated, but only walked six feet before stopping, turning around and making eye contact with me again.

"He wants us to follow him," River whispered.

Since I wasn't exactly overloaded with alternative ideas, I began to follow the creature. He led us into one of the orchards, then across it toward the other side of the atrium, along the veranda, until we reached the small room that held the entrance to the prison down in the basement.

The leopard approached the door to the room and nudged it with his head. It had been ajar, and now swung open slowly. He stepped inside, and I followed, maintaining about three feet between us. The small bare room was dark, as it usually was. The leopard stopped in front of the heavy door on the opposite side of the room that led to the prison and perched on his hind legs.

"What's he doing?" River whispered.

I had no idea, but I was beginning to regret following this animal. I feared that we were just wasting our time.

The door was locked, as it always was. There wasn't any sign of the key in the room. I didn't know why this animal wanted to lead us down into the human dungeon. For all I knew, he wanted us to feed them.

"Let's go," I said, breathing out in frustration.

There was a sharp click the moment I turned my back on the creature.

"Look," River gasped.

She craned her neck behind us. I turned around to see the door had clicked open, and was now being pushed against by the leopard. He nudged the door, then pushed it open wide with his agile body, before sitting on the other side of the doorway, resuming that same calm, patient position.

Now this cat had my full attention.

I had no clue how the door had unlocked like that. I half expected to see someone standing on the other side as we stepped through, but there was no one. Just the leopard. Once we had stepped through the doorway, the animal began heading down the staircase, leading us down to the basement.

The scent of human blood consumed me. I was about to reach for River's wrist to breathe her in when she anticipated my move and pressed it against my nose.

We weaved around the cells, following this odd animal, through chamber after chamber. I didn't dare to look through the windows of the cells as we passed by them. I didn't want to make the temptation any greater to burst into one of the rooms and embark on a murdering spree.

I'd explored this place a few times before, but I'd never had time to venture so deep into this huge maze of tunnels. Soon we had reached an area that I'd never been in before. Even though I'd suspected that there was a lot more to this prison than I had seen, I hadn't expected it to be quite this large. The leopard's pace quickened, enabling us to pass through quicker. Finally, once I began to doubt that we could even go any deeper, the leopard stopped outside another door. Again, there was a click and it popped open.

We entered after the leopard into a small storage

room of sorts. There was a trapdoor in the center of the room, and a pile of sacks heaped in one corner, with an odd sprinkling of white powder on the floor. Otherwise there was nothing too remarkable here, just some brooms, mops and other cleaning equipment, and a cupboard fixed against the opposite wall. The leopard crossed the room and walked right up to the piece of furniture. He moved around to the back of it. Squeezing his head between the gap between the back of the cupboard and the wall, he made it larger as he pushed against it before squeezing his whole body through the crevice.

At this point, I put River back down on her feet because we both wouldn't fit through. Positioning myself sideways, I moved through the narrow gap after the leopard and was amazed to see that behind the cupboard was another door that the leopard had just disappeared through. I slipped through it myself and found myself at the top of a dark, winding staircase. I caught sight of the leopard's tail disappearing around a corner a few flights down.

I heard River's shallow breathing behind me. Her

hand slid into mine and gripped it. Her bright eyes grew wide as she stared down at the secret staircase.

"What in the world…" she murmured.

She met my eyes for a few seconds before we hurried down after the leopard.

We turned corner after corner until I was beginning to feel dizzy from the turning. Then we reached the last step.

We had appeared in some kind of kitchen. Although kitchen seemed an insulting word. It was the largest, most opulent kitchen I'd ever seen. A crystal—or was it diamond?—chandelier hung from the high ceiling. The floors were made of a sleek black stone, and piled atop gold-plated tables were plates and cutlery made of what appeared to be solid silver. There was a fragrant scent of exotic spices, the remains of cooking that couldn't have been done more than a few hours ago.

What is this place?

The leopard was already halfway across the room. River and I had been so dumbstruck, we'd remained standing, just looking around the room. But the animal was moving faster than ever now, so we hurried to catch up with him.

We exited the kitchen, and, stepping outside, I was shocked to find myself looking out over another atrium. An atrium that made the beautiful one up above seem characterless and basic. The sheer scale of it made my head reel, and there was barely an inch of it that wasn't decorated with precious gems and metals. In the center, there were sprawling gardens that looked like they belonged in heaven. Dozens of pure white swans floated upon a sparkling lake. Pink flamingos stood on its bank, and there was an array of other tropical birds emitting a symphony of chirping as they fluttered from tree to tree, their feathers bright. A light mist hung over the place, and a heady aroma of flowers tinged the atmosphere. A pleasant, mild breeze touched my skin—from where it came I had no idea.

"Wow," River breathed against my ear.

Again, River and I couldn't stand admiring for long. The leopard had continued on his way along one of the verandas. To our left, it appeared that we were passing along residences of some sort—apartments, just as there had been in the atrium above. Only the closed doors gave me a glimpse of what magnificence must be on the inside. Made of dark wood, they were carved with floral patterns and studded with a myriad of gems.

As we made our way along the veranda, I took in as much of this place as I could. Leaving aside the grand scale and opulence of it, it appeared quite similar in structure to the one above. Although from what I could see, there didn't appear to be any elevators.

The leopard led us to a flight of wide stairs covered with a maroon carpet.

We climbed up and reappeared on a level that was just as beautiful as the last. But the leopard did not venture out onto this one. He remained on the staircase, leading us higher and higher until we had reached the very top level of the atrium. As soon as we stepped out onto it, it was clear that this held an even grander scale of opulence—if that was possible. My eyes popped at the attention to detail. Even the doorknobs appeared to be encrusted with what looked like… diamonds. It was mind-blowing to even begin considering how much wealth was in this place. It would be an inconceivable sum.

Finally, the leopard stopped again outside what appeared to be the grandest door of the whole place. I expected it to click open just as all the other doors had. But this one didn't. Instead, the leopard stood on his hind legs and reached up to knock a bell with his front right paw. A rich chime sounded out, and then there was silence.

River held her breath, her grip tightening around my hand. I was surprised when the doorknob turned and the door opened. I hadn't heard any footsteps leading up to it.

As the door swung fully open, I almost choked.

Chapter 11: River

An unearthly vision appeared before our eyes. The top half of an impossibly beautiful woman floated upon a whirl of pale blue mist. She had stunning golden eyes and curling jet-black hair that trailed past her waistline. Her jawline was strong and she had wide, thick lips. A richly embroidered azure bandeau adorned her chest, revealing her muscled lower stomach. Her ivory skin shimmered in the soft lighting of the corridor, making her appear all the more ethereal.

When she opened her mouth to speak, it was in a familiar voice. A voice that was soft and silky, yet so distinct that it rang in my ears as though she was shouting. It was a voice that had appeared in my head before, and I was sure in Ben's too.

"Welcome home."

Ben and I were both lost for words. I was beyond thinking that I must be dreaming, but the sight of this—woman? Ghost? I didn't even know what to call her—it was just too much for my mind to process.

As if I wasn't already struggling enough, the leopard walked right up to the woman, and a second later, he'd transformed into a man... at least, the top half of a man. He had warm brown hair and orange eyes, and the bottom half of him consisted only of smoke, just like the woman. Also like the woman, he had a thick jaw, although it was far more pronounced than hers. He cast his orange gaze toward Ben and me briefly before turning to the woman. Placing one hand beneath her chin, he leaned in and caught her lips in his.

The woman smiled like a cat as he drew away. A

contented expression on her face, she looked back at us. "Thank you for fetching them, Bahir." As she looked Ben and me over, her eyes remained longer on me, her smile broadening—or perhaps it was just my imagination.

Bahir glanced our way once more, then vanished, leaving us alone with the woman.

"Come in," she said, beckoning us inside.

Ben remained rooted to the spot, holding me there with him. He found his voice before me. "Who are you?"

A gust of wind appeared out of nowhere behind us. The unexpected force of it pushed us both forward, through the doorway and into the woman's corridor.

The front door closed.

Ben's arm found my waist as he held me protectively against him.

"An understandable question," the woman said, still smiling broadly, revealing a set of thick white teeth. "But why don't you make yourself comfortable first, my children?"

Children?

She levitated along the corridor. I looked nervously at Ben. He looked uncertain, but he led us forward, following the woman. When we reached the end of the corridor, we arrived in what appeared to be a living room. It was the size of a hall. Lush green plants in golden pots lined the walls, and embroidered love seats and huge cushions were scattered about. All the fabric I laid eyes on—from the drapes that hung from the walls to the seating material—appeared to be silk, and beaded with pearls or some kind of precious jewel. She led us to an enormous sofa in the center of the room, whose cushions were so big and bouncy they looked like I might get lost in them.

Why do they have so many seats when they don't even have butts? I couldn't help but wonder.

She gestured toward the couch, but Ben didn't sit down. He remained standing, and although my knees felt weak, I remained standing too.

The woman crossed her arms over her chest, her smile fading slightly. "Very well," she said, her face taking on a more serious expression. "You asked who

I am. My name is Nuriya, Queen of the Nasiri Jinn and Mistress of The Oasis."

Jinn.

I looked toward Ben. I wondered if he had even been aware that such creatures existed. From the look on his face, it didn't appear that he had.

My mouth was so dry it hurt to swallow. "What have you done with our people?" I managed. "And my family?"

When her eyes returned to me again, I was surprised to see a flicker of what appeared to be kindness behind them.

"You need not fear for them, my beauty," she said. "They are all quite safe."

"Where are they?" Ben demanded, his fists clenched.

Nuriya looked unamused by Ben's tone of voice. She turned her attention back on me, ignoring his question.

"You want to see your family, dear?" she asked, and for the first time, she touched me. Her fingers brushed against my cheek. They were so soft and smooth, they felt like petals gliding against my skin. I was surprised that I could feel her touch at all. Her body seemed so ethereal, I expected her to just go right through me.

"Where have you taken them?" I asked.

"Come with me." She held out her hand. Eyeing Ben nervously, I reached out and took it. Ben motioned to follow, but she held up a hand to him. "No, Benjamin. You wait here. Your turn will come."

Before he could object, she was pulling me across the hall, toward a door at the other end of it.

Ben sped up. "You're not taking her away from me," he said, grabbing my arm.

"Ben," I said through gritted teeth. "Let me go. Please."

We didn't know anything about these creatures, and we ought not try their patience—especially when they held our families' lives in their hands. Assuming Nuriya wasn't lying when she said that they were still alive.

Ben must've sensed the desperation in my eyes. He exhaled sharply, then let go of me, his eyes still on me as Nuriya led me through the door. She closed it behind us. We had appeared in a warmly lit corridor.

My heart was pounding in my chest. Would she really be leading me to my family? Or could this be some kind of horrible trap?

Either was equally possible. But now I'd made the decision to face whatever was up ahead of me alone, without Ben, whom I'd come to depend on as my rock.

We arrived outside another door. She pushed it open and glided inside the room. This was clearly a bedroom. Although much smaller than the living room we'd just left, it was still excessively large. So large that as my eyes traveled from one end to the other, it took several moments before I realized that it was not empty. A tall man stood by the edge of a double bed.

A young man.

My older brother.

My voice caught in my throat.

"J-Jamil!"

I rushed forward and pulled him into an embrace.

He hugged me back. I took a step back. Looking up at his face, I realized that something was very, very different.

First of all, he was standing the way... a normal person would. His posture was straight and upright, his arms at his sides. And his expression, it was abnormally lucid.

"River," he said.

My jaw dropped at the way he said my name. Perfectly pronounced, with such an even tone of voice.

I narrowed my eyes, scrutinizing his face. I barely believed what I was seeing.

"Jamil?" I breathed. "What happened to you?"

A frown knotted his dark brows. "I... I'm not quite sure."

A chill ran down my spine. It was impossible to describe what it felt like to speak with my nineteen-year-old brother for the first time in my life. Not speaking *to* him. Speaking *with* him. To hear him respond to my words. To know that he heard and understood me. To not be in doubt as to what he was trying to communicate.

I was living the dream that had recurred so many nights in my sleep during the past weeks, ever since I had been given that vial of amber liquid.

Tears welled in my eyes. Since the discovery that my family had gone missing I'd been fighting to control my emotions, but now I couldn't hold them back. Tears flooded down my cheeks like streams, and I turned into a blubbering mess as I wrapped my arms around Jamil's neck and hugged him tighter, as if I'd never let go.

I sobbed harder as he hugged me back again.

"You have no idea what this feels like," I breathed. "I-It's like I'm meeting you for the first time."

"I do, River." His hands moved up to my shoulders and he clutched them. Creating some distance between us, he looked down at me to reveal tears in his own eyes.

He looked in a daze, utterly overwhelmed. I couldn't even begin to imagine what he was feeling. I'd learned lots about what it was like to suffer from autism from sitting in on doctors' appointments and also from my mother's own research in the field, but it was still impossible to comprehend what he'd been through all those years. Now, to suddenly be normal, it must have felt like… a new birth.

He was speechless for several minutes. He just remained gaping down at me, as though still trying to process his own mind.

The door to the bedroom shut behind us. Nuriya had given us some privacy. I was not sure if she had even entered the room in the first place. As soon as I'd seen my brother standing by the bed, I'd become completely oblivious to her presence.

Jamil ran his pale hands over his face, and I was once again struck by how much he looked like my father, especially now that his facial expressions were normal.

"It's like I… don't know myself," he said slowly. "I don't know who I am. What I am."

I was amazed that he even had a vocabulary. His condition had been so severe, he had never been able to have a proper education. I wondered if all the times he'd heard our conversations at home, our language had slipped into his subconscious and now he was able to summon it. But I doubted that. For one thing, his speech was too perfect. This was like… magic.

I wiped my eyes with the back of my wrist, then smiled and squeezed his hand.

"Don't worry, Jamil. You'll find yourself. I'll help you. We all will. We'll figure out together a way for you to build up your life afresh…"

But first, we need to get out of here.

A chirping erupted near the bed. I cast my eyes toward the noise. A golden bird cage held a single white dove. The bird appeared to have just woken, and had begun to beat its wings against the cage.

"Where are Mom, our sisters and Grandpa?" I asked, turning back to my brother.

Jamil shook his head. "I don't know."

"What's the last thing you remember?"

He wrinkled his nose in memory. "I was at home, in my bed. Mom had just gotten me ready to sleep. That's the last thing I remember."

"You don't remember anyone feeding you some

kind of amber liquid from a vial? You just woke up in this room, like this?"

He nodded.

Wow. This must have been more bewildering for him than I'd thought.

"Okay," I said, taking a deep breath. "We're going to have to try to find our family."

"What is this place?" he asked.

I paused, biting my lip. I wasn't sure if he had even come face to face with any jinn yet. He was overwhelmed as it was, beginning to explain to him about the world of supernaturals... It was just far too much at this point.

I didn't want to lie to him, but I was not sure that he could handle the truth. I fumbled for words, wondering what to tell him, as he watched me closely.

One option was to tell him that we had been kidnapped, but that was no less alarming. I just tried to be as truthful as possible without completely blowing his fragile mind.

"We're in Egypt, near Cairo," I said. "I'm not sure

why you woke up in this room. I've been away from everyone for a while…" I wasn't sure if he'd been able to follow what was happening, or remembered. It seemed that he hadn't, because he raised a brow as though it was news to him. "I got into some trouble recently… Look, Jamil. It's complicated but I promise I'm going to give you a full explanation. For now, just know that I'm not entirely sure how or why you're here. I just know that I need to help you get out."

He nodded slowly, wetting his lower lip. "Okay, and how do we do that?"

"I'm going to try to find out. But while I do, I think it's best that you stay in this room."

To my surprise, he winced. Then he reached for his right upper arm. He pulled up the sleeve of his T-shirt to reveal the tattoo of a black cross.

Oh, no.

"And do you know what this is?" he asked, grimacing. "It's stinging like hell. I have no idea how it got there, or who put it on me. I just woke up with it."

As much as my heart was still bursting with more joy than I knew how to handle over Jamil's miraculous recovery, I couldn't help but feel a building sense of dread. My eyes traveled nervously to the dove still flapping about in the small ornate cage.

In this strange, wondrous place called The Oasis, I doubted there was anything that came without a price.

CHAPTER 12: BEN

I hated to watch River leave me, but I gave in to her request. I understood. We were at these creatures' mercy, and aggravating them would only work against us.

And so I remained waiting in that massive living room. Although I didn't sit. I kept pacing up and down, waiting for River and Nuriya to return.

To my dismay, the jinni returned alone. Her golden eyes fixed on me as she floated across the room.

"Now, Benjamin," she said softly. "I'm all yours."

"Where's River?" I asked, my stomach clenching.

"She's just in the other room, with her brother."

"Her brother?"

"Yes. We cured his illness."

I stared at her, wondering if anything coming out of her mouth was truthful.

"In fact," she said, "one of our gifts to River when she arrived was a cure to her brother's illness. Along with wealth to solve her mother's woes. She just took her time in giving them, so I decided to do what was in her interest and give them to her family myself."

"How did you know about River's family?"

A smile curled the corners of her lips. "We are jinn, Benjamin. We make it our business to learn about our serfs. It's our responsibility."

Serfs. That's what they see us as.

"We provided gifts to you, too," she continued, "but perhaps you didn't realize it. As much human blood as you wanted, without having to make the kill yourself. Is that not what you desired so passionately when you arrived here?"

I couldn't deny that it was. It had been the only thing on my mind at the time—to be able to have an unlimited supply of blood without needing to commit murders myself and lose myself further in the darkness.

"Then we watched over you even after you decided to leave us," she said. "During your time away, we made sure you had ample blood and protected both of you from danger."

That would explain a lot.

So these creatures are some kind of mystic mind readers. How extensive their mental powers were, I couldn't be sure. But it was clear to me that these tattoos they etched into each of their "serfs" forged a close connection between them and us.

Jeramiah had a tattoo, along with all the other vampires and half-bloods I saw. They too must be servants to the jinn.

"Where is my family?" I demanded once again.

"I told you already, they are here. And they are safe. And they shall remain safe. Because they are under our care now, they, too, are my responsibility."

"What do you mean exactly by responsibility?"

"I mean we take care of our own."

"Neither I, River, her family nor any of my people are your own," I snapped.

Amusement played across her face. "Anyone who seeks out The Oasis becomes our own. Desiring The Oasis means desiring our home, which in turn means desiring us... which means we desire you."

This woman is insane.

Clearly, she was living in a different reality to me, a reality I needed to understand and learn the rules of if I was to get us all out of this mess.

"I see," I said, although I saw nothing. I was trying to reel in my temper. "So you consider us your serfs?"

She chuckled. "Yes and no. You are serfs, and yet you are also much more than that to me, my child. You are part of our family." Before I could stop her, she leaned down and pressed her petal-like lips against my forehead in a tender kiss before drawing away again. "We take pleasure in fulfilling the desires of our loved ones, as you will come to take pleasure in fulfilling ours... You may address me as Mother, if you like."

This conversation was becoming more absurd by the sentence.

One mother is enough for me, thanks.

"So," I said, trying to follow her line of logic, "if you see me as your family—indeed, as your son—and you want to make me happy, I'm telling you what would make me very happy. Free River, her family, my family and everyone else you swiped from the desert in the last hour."

Her smile grew wider, revealing more of her thick pearly-white teeth. "We are wish-fulfillers, my love. But there is also such a thing as deserving before desiring. We are generous to new arrivals, since you are first coming into our fold and getting used to a new way of life. But after that, you must be deserving of the wishes you ask for. Letting loose all those newcomers, that's a very, very heavy request. Certainly, you are not deserving of it right now, but even if I agreed to grant it to you in advance of your earning it… I'm not certain that you are ready to bear the burden of deserving such a thing."

So there's the catch. Twisted creature.

"So tell me," I said, gritting my teeth, "is there a way I can deserve it?"

She paused, looking me over from head to foot. Then a glint of what appeared to be excitement sparked in her eyes.

"Of course, there's something you could do. Although it's never been done before, since before now we've not come across anyone who desired so much from us, but if you're determined… we could form a bond deeper with you than anyone has ever formed with us before. Which would grant you not only freedom of River's family and those we took from the desert in the last hour, but also an unlimited number of wishes from us."

I paused. "What exactly does this involve? What would be the difference between this bond you speak of and the hold that you already have over me?" I asked.

"Even with the bond we share now, if you decided that you hated your life here, and you wanted to leave your new family, you could earn freedom. In fact, that is what some vampires here have been working toward for the past few decades—cutting down on the things they desire while here in The Oasis and doing us extra favors… But you… if we went a level deeper with our bond, you would be eternally indebted to us. A soul bound to serve the Nasiri family for life. Although you could ask us for anything else you wanted, and we would fulfil it as long as it was within our powers, you could never ask for freedom, no matter what you did to deserve it."

My mouth dried out. It was hardly a wonder why nobody had ever entered into such a contract.

Selling myself as a slave to these creatures for the rest of my immortal existence.

There must be some other way.

"Why were we allowed to leave The Oasis before?" I asked. "River and me. Jeramiah allowed us to just leave. Why was that if we supposedly did not deserve it?"

The queen let out a soft chuckle. "But you never truly left, did you?"

The truth dawned on me. Of course, the presence

of The Oasis had been with us the whole time. River had even remarked after hearing the echoing in her ears that it had been like we'd never left.

"The reason I let you go," Nuriya continued, "was because sometimes it takes time for loved ones to realize what is best for them. I wanted you to experience what life was like without us, and realize the richness of the life you could experience here... where anything is possible."

"That vision I had," I said quietly, my eyes boring into hers. "Me as an infant. In Aviary. You gave that to me, didn't you?"

"Yes," she said, placing a hand on my shoulder. "As I've been trying to get you to understand, we can help you in ways nobody in the world can. Not even your own flesh and blood."

I sat down in the chair nearest to me and covered my face in my hands.

My personal problems and the mystery about myself that I'd been so desperate to solve—all of this was the last thing on my mind now.

All I could think about was my family, River and

everyone else I'd led here. And the responsibility I had to free them. Their imprisonment here was all my fault. If I hadn't taken up Jeramiah's suggestion in Chile to come here to begin with, none of this would've happened. I was the one who'd sparked these events, and now I had to do whatever it took to get them out of it.

I'd had more than enough experience of the jinn's influence over the past weeks to not be foolish enough to believe that any of us could escape without their permission. That there was any other way to set them free than to agree to this jinni's proposal. She was the one who ran this place and decided who came and left. Heck, she even had Jeramiah under her thumb.

The situation seemed utterly farfetched and downright insane, but the thought of where my family could be right now and what the jinn could possibly be doing to them was eating away at any reason and logic my panic-stricken brain still possessed.

When I looked back up at Nuriya, waiting for my decision, there were only two words on my mind:

"I agree."

CHAPTER 13: RIVER

After sitting with my brother for a few more minutes, I needed to go back to Ben. We had to figure out how we were going to escape this place with our families. I moved to the door, but as I touched the handle, it moved and clicked open. I moved back. To my surprise, Ben stepped into the room.

I was instantly struck by his expression. It was strangely calm. More calm than I remembered seeing him for a long time. My heart lifted, wondering if he could have somehow come up with a solution while I'd been in here with Jamil.

"What happened?" I asked, staring at him.

His eyes fixed on mine intensely. "I found a way out," he said, his voice low and deep.

"What do you mean?"

"I found a way to free us all."

"How?"

"Just follow me."

My heart pounding in my chest, I turned around to Jamil, who was staring at Ben with curiosity.

"Jamil, this is my friend Benjamin. You heard him, he's going to help us get out of here."

My brother stepped forward to approach, but Ben immediately shot backward. In my relief to see Ben, I'd forgotten what danger he posed to my brother.

"It's good to meet you, Jamil," Ben said from a distance.

"And you too," Jamil said, looking confused by Ben's behavior and still completely out of his depth.

I turned back to Ben. "So do you know where my family is? And your family? The witches? Everyone else?"

I could hardly suppress the relief and excitement bubbling up within me. Despite the fact that I still didn't understand how on earth Ben had managed to pull this off, right now, I didn't have bandwidth in my buzzing mind to think too much. All I could think about was seeing the rest of my family again, escaping this place, and returning to The Shade with them.

"Come with me," Ben said. I grabbed hold of Jamil's hand, and we followed Ben out of the room.

In the corridor outside, to my dismay, a jinni was waiting there for us. Not Nuriya—a male jinni. This man bore much resemblance to the queen herself. He shared the same jet-black curly hair and stiff jawline, and the noble shape of his nose was also much like hers.

Jamil's eyes looked like they were about to pop from their sockets as he gaped at the creature.

I slid an arm around his waist, worrying that he might even faint from the shock. He must've been thinking that he was in some kind of bizarre dream, and perhaps that was best for him. It would help him to get through all this.

The jinni led us further along the corridor, right until the end, when he stopped outside the door. He pushed it open to reveal another bedroom much like the one Jamil and I had just been in, although larger. It contained three single beds lined up along one side of the wall. Huddled together on one of the beds were my mother, Dafne, and Lalia. My sisters had been holding my mother tightly, their heads buried in her arms, as she sat comforting them with a drained, terrified look on her face. But the moment they noticed Jamil and me, their eyes lit up. Even though the jinni was present next to us, the three of them leapt off the bed and rushed toward us.

A huge smile spread across my face as I waited for the penny to drop.

My mother gasped as she clutched Jamil. She was staring up at his face as though she needed glasses, squinting and touching his face.

"Jamil?" she breathed. "Are you okay?"

My heart soared as he replied with perfect pronunciation, "Yes, Mom. I'm okay. I don't know how, but... I'm feeling better than I ever remember."

My mother looked from my brother to me, then back to my brother. She cupped his face in her hands, her mouth opening and closing like a fish. She was utterly speechless for several moments before emotions overtook her and she broke down sobbing against his chest.

I picked Lalia up as she flung herself at me. Wrapping her legs around my waist and her arms around my neck, she planted slobbery kiss after kiss on my cheek, holding me so tight she was practically strangling me.

Dafne was rooted to the spot, her face pale with shock, staring at me and Jamil as though we were both strangers.

When my mother drew away from Jamil, she was shaking.

"What happened?" she wheezed, moving to me and hugging me as much as she could while Lalia hogged me.

"We don't have time to explain now, Mom," I said.

"My God, River. You're so cold! What's wrong, honey? Are you ill?"

"I'm okay. I'm not ill. I've just… got a lot to tell you. But where's Grandpa?" I looked around the room again.

"I-I don't know," my mother replied. "When I heard you'd gone missing, I brought Jamil to Cairo and stayed with your grandfather, Dafne and Lalia in his house. The day we were brought… here… your grandfather had gone out. It was just the four of us at home. A strange mist filled the place and it seemed to knock us all unconscious. When we woke up, we were in this room. I thought we'd been gassed but—"

"Okay," I said, hating to interrupt her. As much as I was dying to hear the full story, we had to get a move on. I looked at the jinni. "Was my grandfather brought here too?"

The jinni shook his head.

Thank God. My family and I shared the same look of relief. I wasn't sure if his elderly heart could have taken the fright. He'd been under enough stress as it was recently.

I nodded toward Ben, who'd remained as far away as possible and was watching our reunion from the doorway.

"This is Ben, my friend," I said to my mother, deliberately leaving out the fact that he was a vampire as I'd done with Jamil. They'd find out soon enough. "He's found a way to get us all out of here."

Here. My mother didn't even know where here was.

Her, Lalia's and Dafne's gazes fell on Ben. His stoic expression broke as he offered them a slight smile. I could see how nervous he felt about being so close to my human family. I had to keep a close eye on him. If he showed even the slightest sign of moving toward us, I'd rush at him and smother him.

"Let's go to your family now, Ben," I said.

He nodded.

Still carrying Lalia, who clung to me like a monkey, I took Dafne's clammy hand, as well as my mother's. My mother had latched onto Jamil again.

I would never know what this experience had been like for my mother. She'd spent the last nineteen years of her life raising an intensely sick son, fully expecting to continue caring for him until she died. She'd held not even a glimmer of hope that he'd ever live a normal life—or even a life without pain and suffering. A life that most people took for granted. Now, seeing her child changed—normal for the first time, the way she'd wished he always was— it was no wonder she was shaking. She was still in shock, and I expected it to take a long time before the reality fully sank in.

The jinni hovered up ahead of us with Ben, and we followed them out into the corridor and then took a left. My family stared around in wonder as we reentered the grand living room of Nuriya's apartment. It was empty now, and the male jinni led us right across it toward another door at the far end of it. This led us into another corridor, at the end of which was the exit to the apartment. We stepped through it, emerging back out into the magnificent atrium where he led us down the wide, carpeted staircase and all the way back to the kitchen. This huge room was also empty, but now there were some pots cooking on the giant stove. I'd no idea what they were cooking, but the fragrance coming from the pots was so divine it made my mouth water.

Ben hadn't said a word yet about where his family and the others were being kept, but as we began climbing up the winding staircase leading back to the atrium above, I could only conclude that they'd been put up there and not in the jinn's atrium like my family.

I thought about all The Shade's inhabitants we were about to meet. Yet more supernatural creatures to blow my family's mind. I was interested in particular in my mother's reaction. She had always been the most skeptical person in the world, not believing anything she saw on the television. Now, in the midst of this supernatural world, I could already see it was doing her head in.

As we passed through the prison cells housing humans and newly half-turned vampires, my family's expressions turned to horror. Especially Lalia, who'd been trapped down here with Hassan. Her whole body tensed up and she buried her head against my neck. She closed her eyes, gripping me even tighter.

I pressed my lips against her soft cheek. "It's okay, Laly. We're leaving this place."

We passed through the last of the sprawling network of prison chambers and climbed up the steps toward the exit. The jinni opened the door, allowing Ben to step through first before we followed, arriving in the familiar bare room.

We stepped out into the gardens in the center of the atrium—which now appeared tame and ordinary compared to the heaven beneath us. We walked along the veranda and stopped outside the seventh door to our left. There were murmurs coming from inside—indicating a crowd.

As Ben pushed open the door and we stepped inside a large dining hall of sorts, gasps swept around the room. To my relief, it seemed that the whole crowd of people we had arrived with had been bundled in here… except I couldn't make out any witches. There was a long table down the center of it, and dozens of chairs dotted about. Some were sitting, but most were standing, with tight expressions on their faces.

Sofia rushed up to Ben, and Derek looked like he wanted to, but held back to avoid tempting his son with his blood. Sofia clutched her son, even as her eyes roamed my family and finally settled on the jinni.

"What's happening?" she and her husband asked at once.

"I found a way out," Ben replied, looking over the crowd as well as his parents. "You all need to come with us. Now."

I was surprised that Ben didn't ask what had happened to them exactly. Perhaps Nuriya or this jinni had already told him, or he'd just guessed that they would've been kept here in this room the whole time. Why exactly the jinn had taken them, I still didn't understand.

But as before, now wasn't the time for questions. Now was the time for escape. I knew that Ben would fill us all in as soon as we arrived back in The Shade.

The Shade. Thinking of that island again, I could hardly contain my excitement as I imagined returning there with my family and showing them around. The spellbound looks on their faces…

"We just need to fetch the witches now," Ben said, "and then we can get out of here."

Derek appeared uneasy as he looked his son over, but he didn't say anything. The room emptied as they followed us back out. Stepping out into the gardens, I wondered where the jinn were keeping the witches.

I was surprised when the jinni stopped outside a towering silver birdcage erected in the middle of a willow-tree grove. It was filled with bright blue parrots who were fluttering about in unrest. I couldn't ever remember seeing this while staying here, nor even on Ben's and my way down just an hour or so ago.

The jinni raised a hand, and with a snap of his

fingers, the birds' wings arrested in midair and they drifted in slow motion downward. Almost as soon as their bodies touched the ground, a billow of smoke appeared from nowhere and engulfed the entire cage. As it cleared, I found myself staring at a cage filled with our witches. Their faces were pale and they looked utterly traumatized. Ibrahim was standing near the front, his white knuckles gripping the bars. He glared at the jinni, who barely made eye contact with any of them. The jinni casually moved to the entrance of the cage, opened the door and let them pile out.

"We're ready to leave now," Benjamin said, eyeing everyone as though the sight we had just witnessed was nothing out of the ordinary. Apparently, he'd been expecting it. "Now we head up to the desert."

There were far too many of us to fit in the elevators, so I wondered how exactly we were going to get up there. Whether or not the witches had their powers intact to vanish us, or perhaps the jinni himself would…

My question was answered as the black-haired

jinni turned on Ben. "You don't need me anymore. You know the way out."

With that, he vanished, leaving a thin veil of light blue mist behind him.

Ben addressed the witches. "You can transport us above ground," he said. "But only above ground— not beyond the boundary yet. All right?"

I was confused why Ben would request this. If we had been given permission to leave, why didn't we just get right out of The Oasis and return straight to The Shade before the jinn changed their minds? I didn't understand why he wanted us to hang around in the desert upstairs. Still, Ben appeared too sure of himself for any of us to question it.

And so each of us gathered together and formed a circle. The witches magicked us out of the atrium and we reappeared up in the desert. The heat was stifling. Compared to the chambers below, it hit me like a wave. Although I was grateful for the change. My bones had begun to ache again while down there. It was too cool for my comfort.

I caught my mother's and siblings' eyes. They

looked at me as though they were dying for an explanation, but mostly, I saw sheer relief in their eyes to be away from the underground and out in the open.

"All right." Ben spoke up. "We've been given permission to go outside the boundary…" He paused. I was surprised when his voice caught in his throat. For the first time, his calm demeanor wavered, giving way to a look of… sadness? His gaze passed from his father, to his mother, to his sister, uncle, and then traveling over everyone else who was present.

His hesitation was leaving me ill at ease.

"What is it, Ben?" I whispered, tugging on his arm.

Finally his eyes fell on me. And something sparked in them. His gaze increased in intensity and there was a look of urgency in his green eyes as they dug into mine.

I frowned in confusion. I parted my lips, once again about to ask him what was wrong.

But before I could utter a single word, his lips

were on mine. His kiss was hungry, passionate, more demanding than ever before. All-consuming. He claimed my mouth so entirely, I couldn't even gasp for breath. His tongue pushed between my lips, his hands gripping my hair roughly as he held my face against his.

By the time he pulled away, I was breathless and my lips felt swollen and bruised.

But more than anything, I felt panic.

I didn't even understand why, but I wanted to stop everything that was happening. I wanted to freeze time, stop Ben when he turned to the crowd and said, "Okay. Let's form a circle."

Something was wrong, very wrong with Ben. And I didn't want anything else to happen until I figured out what. But he didn't give me a chance to say anything. He grabbed my hand, holding it firmly, and hurried everyone into a circle.

He shot a look at Ibrahim and nodded sharply.

I didn't know how I realized what was about to happen next, but all at once, I just knew.

Ben was going to let go of my and his mother's

hand a split second before we vanished.

I had barely seconds to process the thought after it entered my head. But when Ben's hand loosened from mine just as we were on the cusp of vanishing back to The Shade, I didn't even need to think what to do.

As though it was instinct, my own hand loosened from my mother's.

Chapter 14: River

I'd never seen Ben look so horrified as the moment he realized what I had just done.

"River," he gasped.

Then his expression turned to anger. He grabbed my shoulders, painfully, and shook me. "What the hell did you just do?"

His own anger ignited a fire within me. Planting my palms flat against his chest, I pushed with all the strength I could muster, forcing him backward a few steps.

"What do you mean what the hell did I just do? What the hell did *you* just do?"

An unexpected fury was boiling up within me. The thought that he was just going to leave us all like that, without so much as an explanation... Leave me.

My throat felt tight as I grabbed hold of his shirt and twisted its fabric in my fists.

"Why, Ben?" I croaked.

His hands closed around mine, detaching me from his shirt and lowering my hands until he was just holding them in his.

"You shouldn't have let go!" he said, anger and shock still shaking his voice.

"What did you expect me to do?"

He looked at me like I was a fool. "Hold on! What idiocy possessed you to let go of your mother's hand?"

I glared up at him, wanting to shoot back a retort, but finding myself asking the same question. *What idiocy did possess me? Why did I let go of my mother's hand?*

I still didn't know why I had reacted the way I had.

It had just seemed like the most natural thing in the world. Like putting one foot in front of the other. There was no way I could explain. Except…

"That idiocy would be you," I replied, my voice quieter this time.

I sensed his temper take a dip. His brows furrowed, a flicker of confusion playing across his face as he stared down at me.

I lowered my eyes to the ground, finding his gaze suddenly too intense, too exhausting, as he studied me. I felt my cheeks grow hot, my breathing shallower.

I still had no idea why he had hung back. But in that moment, it became clear to me that the feelings I held for Ben were far deeper than I had ever thought.

The truth was, the pain of leaving without him far outweighed the fear of leaving my family and staying with him in this place.

I felt almost too embarrassed to admit this to him, because I didn't know if he felt the same strength of emotion for me. After all, he had been prepared to just leave me.

My mouth dried out, and I felt lost as to what to say next. The silence burned my ears as I kicked at the sand beneath my feet. I was relieved when Ben broke it.

"River, I..." He paused. I raised my eyes to his face again to see that he looked less livid, although no less tense. "I had no idea that you'd do that for me."

I hadn't known I would do that myself. Abandon my family for Benjamin Novak? A boy I had only just recently met and whom I still didn't know a lot about? If someone had asked me that question, the logical answer would've been that I would have chosen my family, of course. My mother, brother, two sisters... They were my life, my flesh and blood. And yet it seemed that my brain had stopped responding to logic or reason.

"You've found your family now," Ben continued. "All of them, and even your brother has been cured of his illness. I... I thought you could go back to The Shade and get on with your life. Maybe even turn back into a human and return to New York if The Shade didn't work out for you."

The way he was speaking, revealing that he had been thinking so far into the future—a future without him—sent shivers down my spine.

"Ben, what happened to you?" I managed. "How did you convince the jinn to set us free?"

His face darkened and now it was his turn to avert his eyes.

He inhaled deeply, and I could see that every part of him was reluctant to answer my question.

"I made a deal with them," he said quietly.

My breath hitched. The hold the jinn had over us already was terrifying enough, the thought of a deal made my blood run cold. "What do you mean 'deal'?"

He hesitated. I clutched his arms, squeezing them hard. "What deal, Ben?"

Finally he raised his head and looked directly at me. There was a discomforting acceptance in his expression, a resignation, and that same calm I had detected earlier.

"In exchange for them allowing everyone to go free, I agreed to be bound to them."

"Bound? But... aren't we already bound to them? These tattoos they put on us..." I reached for his sleeve and pulled it up to reveal his upper arm. Except there was no tattoo. Thinking that I'd gotten the wrong side, I checked his other arm. No tattoo either. His skin was pale and smooth, as if there never had been a black cross etched into him. I gaped at him. "Where's your tattoo?"

"Nuriya removed it."

"Huh?" I was feeling more confused by the moment. "Why would she do that?"

He held up his right hand, and for the first time I noticed a thin band of gold fit tightly around his wrist. It was in the shape of a cobra, and, to my horror, it appeared to have been clamped right into his flesh. His skin around the edges of it looked reddish and sore.

"What is this?" I breathed.

"Their way of showing that I have moved up in rank... River, I agreed to be bound to them permanently."

"What?"

"The bond they have with you, and had with me—it wasn't permanent. We could earn our freedom if we played our cards right—albeit after decades of self-control. But this"—he held up his wrist again—"is permanent. Because I've voluntarily agreed to submit to them, the bond is much stronger."

I could hardly believe my ears. "H-How could you do that?"

"I didn't have a choice. I've stayed in this place long enough to know that there's no way out without permission—and even when Jeramiah let us out, we never escaped. We were under the influence of the jinn the whole time. Nobody in this place is free—not even Jeramiah and the other vampires who are allowed to wander outside. This place will always have chains on them. I couldn't have that happen to my family and people who came here to help me. Accepting Nuriya's proposal was my only option... And in return for agreeing to be bound, I've been granted an unlimited number of wishes... except my freedom."

My heart hammered in my chest. *Permanently.* The

word still rang through my head. It almost felt like Ben had just committed suicide. "H-How could you stay here forever?"

He shrugged. "I'm able to venture outside, though I will never truly have freedom. I will always be indebted. That's what this band signifies."

Ben's world had just come crashing down around him. I didn't understand how he could talk so calmly. It gave me a glimmer of hope that perhaps he believed there might be some way out of this for him.

"I can't believe this is the only way," I said, my knees feeling weak. "There must be a way to break free from them. Wh-What would happen if you just took that snake band off you?" Desperation shook my voice.

He almost smirked. "It's not as simple as that. This band is more of a symbol than the actual cause of my bondage. I have no idea whether it's possible to break the bond. All I know is that Nuriya said it wasn't." He paused, eyeing me seriously. "In light of this, River, I think you should reconsider. I think you should leave. It's not too late. I could request the jinn to set you free of the boundary. You could return to The Shade, to your family, and just… get on with your life, dammit."

I shook my head forcefully. "No, Ben. I won't. I can't… I-I can't leave you."

Perhaps it was just my stubbornness and wishful thinking, but I simply could not bring myself to believe that there was no other way. All my life I'd been forced to be resourceful, find ways to do things that I previously thought impossible—part of this was my mother's influence. That was one reason I resented my father so much whenever he said he couldn't give up his addiction. Anyone could do anything. It just took determination, perseverance… and occasionally a bit of luck.

I looked resolutely into Benjamin Novak's piercing green eyes. The eyes of a man I was beginning to believe I couldn't live without.

"I'm staying with you, Ben, whether you like it or not. I swear, we're going to find a way to get you out of this mess."

Chapter 15: Ben

River didn't know how much her words meant to me. As I'd told her, I really had no idea if there would be a way to free myself—and what the price of that freedom might be. Nuriya had indicated to the contrary, but River's strength at a time when I'd felt hopeless, her determination in standing by my side, even though I didn't feel I'd done anything to deserve such loyalty… it left me speechless.

This girl left her family for me.

The idea was still inconceivable, and I realized that

I found her loyalty to me frightening—the hold I seemed to have over her. I couldn't help but feel that it would only cause her pain in the end. Because I was a runaway train. I had no idea what wreck was waiting for me right around the next corner, and the last thing in the world I wanted to do was drag River along with me.

But at least right now, it seemed that she was set in her determination to stay with me. All I could do was make sure that her stay was as painless as it could be and do all within my power to make sure she stayed safe.

Sliding my hand up her arm, I raised her sleeve to see the black tattoo still etched into her skin. I wasn't sure who and how many of us those jinn had branded, but whoever bore the tattoo was supposed to have had it removed the moment they left the boundary—along with any other bond the jinn had formed with them in the hour they'd been trapped in The Oasis.

Since River had let go of her mother to stay behind the barrier with me, hers still remained. The first thing that I wanted to do now was remove the ugly mark—remove the burning that came with it, and the disquietingly close connection she had with the jinn. Although she wished to stay with me here, I wanted to make her as free as she could possibly be within the confines of the jinn's rule.

I eyed River's beautiful, innocent face once again, and although it made me ache inside, I put my focus back on the entrance to The Oasis.

"Okay," I said, clearing my throat. "If you're sure you're staying, let's go back down now."

Reaching one arm beneath her knees and planting the other firmly around her waist, I picked her up, holding her close against me. I felt more protective of her than ever before. This girl now felt more precious to me than my own life, and if anything happened to her, I would never be able to forgive myself.

As we walked away from the edge of the boundary, across the sand back toward the trap door that led down to the atrium, I pressed my lips against her forehead and kissed her. Once. Twice. Thrice. Soft, slow, gentle kisses. As if I wanted to reassure her that

I wouldn't let her down, even though I had no such reassurance myself. Her cheek pressed against my chest, her arms wrapping around my neck. Her eyes closed tightly.

I wasn't sure what was going through her mind in that moment, as I led her away from freedom and back toward imprisonment, but the intense expression that took over her face as she gripped me harder made it feel like she never wanted to let go of me. She hadn't even asked me where I was going to take her now. What we were going to do next. The way she clung to me... it was as though she was just experiencing relief to be with me. No matter what pit I was about to carry her into.

Leaving the desert and climbing back down the staircase toward the uppermost level, I moved to the edge of the glass wall and peered around to see if any vampires or half-bloods had woken up since we'd been down there. Specifically, I was looking out for my cousin Jeramiah.

So far I could only make out two people—a man and a woman—sitting on a bench in the rose garden.

As the woman turned her head, I realized that she was Marilyn. They were both sipping from cups of steaming liquid and talking in soft tones. I guessed that this was her boyfriend of the week. A fellow half-blood, it seemed.

I was glad that there still weren't many people about. Although Nuriya had accepted River and me back like long-lost children, I doubted anyone else here would be pleased about our return, especially after the way we had left. Bumping into Lloyd in particular would be an uncomfortable experience.

Taking the elevator down to the ground floor, I took a deliberately wide path around where Marilyn and the man were sitting, but she must've sensed my footsteps, because she stood up and spotted River and me.

Her eyes widened as she stared at me. "Hey, Joseph!" she called. I winced at how loud her voice was. "You're back."

I found it odd that Nuriya and the jinn knew and addressed me by my real name, while the others here still apparently thought of me as Joseph. Perhaps the jinn didn't see it as relevant information to reveal to them, but the thought that Jeramiah was living just meters above this knowledge was unnerving. Sooner or later I couldn't help but feel he'd discover my true identity.

I nodded curtly at Marilyn and without saying a word continued with River toward the veranda on the opposite side. When I approached the small room that contained the entrance to the prison below, I stopped outside of it.

I set River down on her feet and reached for the door handle. Although it was locked, the moment I touched it, there was a click and it magically unlocked. This had been another perk of entering a permanent contract with the Nasiris—if it could really be called a perk. I was granted access to their atrium whenever I wanted, and consequently also had access to the human cells. Although I would avoid going there as much as possible. Since I had unlimited wishes, I would request that human blood be delivered to me in jugs so I wouldn't have to go through the trauma of murdering someone. That task would be left to someone else.

We stepped into the bare room, and then I did the same with the second, much sturdier door that protected the prison. It clicked the moment I touched it, and I was able to swing it wide open. Closing my hands around River's, I twined my fingers with hers and guided her inside.

Still, she hadn't asked me what I planned to do next, and so I told her. "In case you haven't guessed already, we're going back down to the Nasiri atrium. The first thing I want to do is get rid of that damned tattoo you still have on you."

"What will that mean exactly?" she asked, as we began to make our way through the maze of prison cells.

"You'll be just like a regular prisoner here. The connection the jinn have with you that allows them to get inside your mind and make you hear and sense things will be removed, and consequently also the brand."

"Okay," she said, casting me a grateful look. "Thank you."

Thank you. She didn't even seem to be aware of how ridiculously inappropriate it was for her to be thanking me. I let it pass.

As we neared the storage room in the deepest part of the prison, she spoke again, "Do you think your family will come back for you?"

"Oh, they will," I replied. "I've no doubt about it. My guess is they'll all return first to The Shade, but then some will come back. Not just for me, but also because my grandfather and his girlfriend are due to arrive here—perhaps they have already—with those three dragons. They'll need to warn him not to try to enter. Of course, none of them will be able to enter without permission, and since I've now forbidden the jinn to touch those they freed again, they'll be forced to return to the island."

"Will you go to see them?" she asked. "Tell them what's happened to you? Even if there's nothing they can do about it, at least it will put their minds at ease."

I grimaced. *Put their minds at ease.* Telling my family that I'd just sold my soul to an ancient clan of jinn would hardly do that, but River was right that at least they would know what had happened to me. And more importantly, I didn't want them hanging around in the desert with the hunters stationed so close by.

"Yes," I replied. "I will have to tell them." By now we had reached the storage room, and were already making our way down the narrow staircase toward the jinn's kitchen. "After we get this tattoo off of you, I'll go back up there. *We'll* go back up there," I added. I didn't want River out of my sight, especially now that we had made enemies in this place. That bastard Michael, for one, would be after her.

We passed through the kitchen where a pile of dirty pots and plates appeared to be washing themselves in the sink, and made our way back up through the atrium toward Nuriya's chambers on the top floor. I knocked on the front door, then stepped back with River, waiting.

When the door opened, it wasn't Nuriya standing behind it. It was another jinni. Female, she looked almost like a younger version of Nuriya. She had the same curling jet-black hair that sprawled down her back and reached to below her waist, but her nose was less straight and more rounded at the tip. Her eyes were amethyst-colored, and her face was rounder and softer, which added to her youthful appearance. Instead of pale blue, beneath her bare abdomen was a light pink smoke.

"Where's Nuriya?" I asked, not bothering to ask who she was exactly.

She eyed me curiously, from head to toe, and then smiled a little before asking, "What do you want her for?" Her voice sounded childish, though from the curve of her waist she was well into adolescence.

Her question grated on my nerves. "Just take me to her, will you?" I said, raising my wrist and showing her the gold band.

"Oh," she said softly. "So you are Benjamin Novak." This jinni only seemed to have eyes for me. I hadn't noticed her once glance at River. "My name's Aisha. Daughter of Karam, and niece of Queen Nuri. I've been delegated to look after you."

I raised a brow. Nuriya hadn't mentioned anything

about delegating the granting of my wishes to someone else. I'd been under the impression that she would grant them herself. This left me unsettled. I didn't know if this girl was as powerful as the queen herself, and after selling my freedom to these creatures, I was going to make damn sure that I received the service I'd paid for.

"As I said," I said, my temper rising, "I would like to see Nuriya."

Aisha cocked her head to one side. Another smile spread across her plump lips. "What's wrong with me?" she asked, a teasing glint in her eyes.

I couldn't believe that a jinni was flirting with me. *This is the last thing I need to deal with right now.*

Tightening my hold on River, I moved to barge right past her, but as I was a step from entering in the doorway, I hit something solid. An invisible barrier. I was forced to step back.

"Listen," she said, an infuriating smirk on her lips. "It seems we've gotten off to a bad start. Why are you so bent on having Nuriya as your wish-granter?"

"Because I have no idea how competent you are," I

steamed.

"Oh, you don't need to worry about that. If there's something that I can't grant you, we'll just go to my aunt. But I am your first point of contact. The queen is very busy, and I'll have much more time for you... much more time."

I could sense River shifting uncomfortably on her feet at the way Aisha was flirting with me so unashamedly.

Clearly, this girl wasn't going to let us through, so I had no choice but to cave in. I moved my hand up River's arm, brushing up her sleeve, and showed the jinni her tattoo.

"I need you to free River from the hold you have over her, and also get rid of this mark you've put on her skin."

Finally, for the first time, the jinni's eyes fell on River. Aisha's lips tightened as her gaze roamed River, almost as though she was sizing River up. Then Aisha looked at her brand.

"Very well," she said. "I can do that... But you are aware that if I do, she would be treated quite differently than the other half-bloods in this place."

I shot the jinni a glare. "What do you mean? She is my girl, and I expect her to be treated not just as well as, but better than any other half-blood in this place."

My girl.

I finally said it.

River's hand squeezed mine a little more tightly.

Aisha shrugged. "Then I suggest that she keeps the tattoo. It's just… a mark that she's one of us. It's only natural that we'd treat one of our own better than an outsider. It also offers her extra protection."

I breathed out sharply, then looked back down at River.

She looked confused as to what to do.

"I… I guess I could just keep it?" she said, shrugging. "I mean, I've kind of gotten used to it by now."

I looked back at the jinni, narrowing my eyes on her. I wondered if it was indeed true that having the mark would mean River was safer. I guessed it made sense, since being bonded meant that she was part of the Nasiri family, and as we'd experienced for ourselves when they'd saved us from those hunters who'd boarded our sub on our journey back to The Shade, these jinn did seem to look out for their own. As much as I was loath to do it, I agreed with River.

"Perhaps you will be safer with it," I muttered.

If River decided to leave me, I could get it removed for her then. But until that time, it seemed that she would remain bonded with these creatures and keep bearing the black mark.

Aisha ran her tongue over her lower lip. "So is there anything else you want from me?"

I heaved a sigh. "Take us back up to the desert. I need to speak to my family."

CHAPTER 16: SOFIA

Ben let go of my hand.

I could hardly believe it when it was happening, and then it was too late. He'd broken off from the circle, and I was transported back to The Shade along with everyone else.

The moment my feet hit solid ground, I lost myself in a panic.

"Ben!" I screamed. "We left him behind!"

Derek's face drained of all color and everyone froze, stunned.

To my surprise, the woman I assumed to be River's mother—for I had not gotten a chance to speak with her yet—was also in hysterics.

"River!" she gasped. "My daughter! I lost my grip on her hand!"

"She let go of you too?" I asked, rushing up to her and grasping her shoulders.

"Let go? I thought she slipped! Why on earth would she let go of me?"

"You need to take us back there now," Derek said to Ibrahim.

"Derek," Ibrahim said, stepping forward, "I'm not going anywhere until I've found my wife. Going back to that place blindly is idiotic—look what almost happened to us! Corrine knows something about that place and I knew we should have waited for her before going there to begin with. I just knew it. I'm going to look for her again now."

"Ibrahim," I said, my voice trembling. "Please. We can't wait that long. Ben, he—"

"Fifteen minutes," Ibrahim said. "Fifteen minutes is all I ask for. If I haven't returned by that time,

Shayla and the other witches can transport you back to The Oasis without me."

I looked at Derek desperately, then back at River's mother, who looked like she was about to hyperventilate.

Although Ibrahim was right that waiting for Corrine's insight might help us, we'd just left my son behind. I didn't know that I could bear waiting more than a minute.

Derek looked torn as Ibrahim vanished from the spot. Then he approached me. Clenching his jaw, he said, "Let's wait fifteen minutes. But not a second longer."

Our hastily assembled army waited with us, making it clear that when we returned, they would all return with us. Although I recognized this, I was in far too much anguish to appreciate their loyalty to us in that moment. All I could think about was my son. *We left him behind. Why did he let go of my hand?* I couldn't even begin to fathom why.

Those fifteen minutes must have been the hardest of my life. I couldn't sit or stand still. I kept pacing up and down, wringing my hands while my insides churned. I could hardly bear to look at Rose. She looked so distraught as she stood near Derek, her fists clenched.

After a quarter of an hour had passed, Ibrahim still hadn't returned.

Derek shot a look at the nearest witches to him—Leyni and Shayla. He gave them a curt nod, and they understood.

Everyone formed a circle once again, and a few seconds later, we were all standing back in the desert.

By now, the heat was unbearable and the blazing sun was high up in the sky, its rays digging into my skin. The witches quickly cast a spell of shadow over all the vampires to keep us protected. Now that I was able to open my eyes without feeling like they were burning, I spotted the three dragons nearby, Jeriad, Neros, and Ridan. Jeriad had one of his heavy wings outstretched, and beneath it stood Kailyn and my father.

On noticing us, Aiden joined us beneath the shade the witches had cast, Kailyn following closely behind him.

"What's happening?" he asked.

My voice felt so choked up, I couldn't handle repeating what had just happened. I was grateful when Derek stepped in. "A lot's happened, none of it good," he said stiffly. Derek proceeded to explain briefly how we'd failed to storm The Oasis, and how Ben and River got left behind.

I could see Aiden and Kailyn's heads were reeling at mention of the jinn—creatures most of us had had no idea even existed until a few hours ago.

Derek and I moved toward The Oasis' boundary, and as we approached it, I began to shout out my son's name.

"Ben! Ben!"

I was beginning to sorely regret having waited fifteen minutes for Ibrahim. God knew where my son was now. Would he even still be up in the desert? Or could he be back down in the atrium? If he was down there, would he be able to hear us? I didn't know if they had some kind of soundproofing around the place. It had certainly sounded quiet down there.

To my relief, my son's voice rang out, loud and deep, to our right.

"I'm here."

"Oh, thank God," I gasped, as my son appeared outside of the boundary. He held a wide black parasol over his head to shield himself from the sun, and standing beside him, her arm looped through his, was River. River's mother and siblings rushed toward her, while the rest of us focused on Ben. I raced up to him, reaching him at the same time as Rose, and we both embraced him.

"Ben!" I choked, smiling through my tears.

I had no idea why he'd stayed behind—perhaps I'd been mistaken, and his hand had simply slipped. And since he had also been holding onto River, perhaps he had accidentally pulled her back with him. Yes, I must have simply misread the situation. But whatever had happened, I didn't care anymore. I'd found my son again, and we'd also found River. Clutching Ben's hand, while Rose held his other, I turned around to face our witches.

"Okay," I said, heaving a sigh of relief. "We can go

now."

Rose and I moved toward the spot where the witches were standing so we could all form a circle again, but to my alarm, Ben didn't budge. He remained rooted to the spot. I whirled around, staring at him.

"Come on," I urged, tugging at him.

His face was ashen as he looked from me, to his sister, and then to his father.

"Come on, Ben!" Rose exclaimed, also pulling at him. Together Rose and I both tugged on him at once, but still, he refused to move.

He slid his hands out of ours, and took a step back.

My heart skipped a beat.

"What's wrong?" I asked, barely breathing.

He shook his head slowly. "I'm sorry," he said. "I can't come with you."

"What?" Derek said. I could see that it took all the self-restraint he had to not rush forward toward Ben also.

"I can't come with you," Ben repeated, his voice strangely—and disconcertingly—calm.

"Why not?" I asked.

He took a deep breath. "I made a deal with the jinn. In exchange for your freedom, I must remain bound to them."

I didn't want to believe what he was saying.

I didn't want to believe that it was true.

"What are you saying?" Rose gasped.

"I mean that I have sold myself to them," Ben replied. "I might still be able to visit The Shade sometimes, but only with permission."

As Ben continued to explain what he'd done, I was barely able to focus on his words. My mind felt numb with despair as I stared at him disbelievingly.

Soon floods of tears were flowing from my eyes. I clasped my son's hand again and began begging him to come back with us, even though he'd just explained why he couldn't. I just wanted it to be untrue. No matter how irrational it was, I wanted him to tell me that everything he'd just said had been a lie—or some kind of sick joke—and that he would return with us to The Shade.

I remained holding onto him, unwilling to let go,

even after he'd finished answering everyone's questions.

Rose approached me, sliding her hands down my arms, slowly detaching me from Ben.

I gulped, my vision blurred as I looked upon my son for the last time for… I didn't know how long.

"I understand why you agreed to the jinn's proposal." Derek spoke somewhere from my right. "And it was a choice you made. But I don't believe there's no way out of this for you, Ben."

"Maybe you're right," Ben replied. "But after what just happened, I don't want you coming near this place anymore and trying to help me. Not you, not Mom, not Rose, not anyone from The Shade… I've done enough damage already."

My heart felt like it shattered into a thousand pieces as he moved further away from us.

I heard the strained voice of River's mother to my left.

"No, River. Please! This makes no sense."

I had been so fixed on my son that I had been oblivious to what was going on between River and her family until now. River's mother had her daughter wrapped tightly in her arms.

"I'm sorry, Mom," River said, her voice subdued. "I just… need to stay with him."

"But why?"

"He… he's my friend. The best I've ever had. You don't know how much Ben has put himself out for me. If it wasn't for him, I doubt I'd even be alive right now. I-I won't be able to live with myself if I don't stay with him."

I was taken aback by River's words. I'd had no idea that she and my son had formed such a strong bond.

She's actually willing to leave her family to stay in The Oasis?

I could hardly believe that she would do that for my son.

Then the truth began to sink in about what must have happened that second before the witches vanished us from the desert.

River must have realized what Ben was doing, and she let go of her mother's hand too.

Despite my grief, I felt a sense of relief. Ben might

not want any of us to stay with him in The Oasis, but at least he seemed to be allowing River to stay with him.

As I stared at the girl continuing to explain with passion to her family why she had to remain by my son's side through this, in this Godforsaken place, I was overcome with affection for her.

As River detached herself from her mother and took a step back, I was unable to stop myself from running up to the girl and pulling her into an embrace. My face still wet from my tears, I kissed her cheeks. Clasping her hands in mine, I looked into her beautiful turquoise eyes.

"Thank you," I breathed.

She gave me a small smile, then hugged me back. I found myself drawing comfort from the firmness of her embrace and when she let go of me, there was a sense of resoluteness in her gaze.

"I promise you, Sofia," she said softly. "I'll do everything I can to help your son."

I bit my lower lip to stop it from trembling. I thought my heart might burst as I experienced an indescribable gratitude for this young woman I barely knew. River could never know how much those words meant to me.

She let go of my hand, then hugged her mother, brother and sisters one more time—wiping the tears from her sisters' cheeks—and then moved toward my son. She slipped her hand into his and then, after one last goodbye, they disappeared within the boundary.

Chapter 17: Ben

Although it had been an agonizing experience facing my family, telling them what I'd done and that I didn't know when I might be able to see them again, it was also strangely liberating. At least now they knew what the situation was.

When I'd first left The Shade, during those months that I was away, it had always played in the back of my mind that my parents didn't know where I was or what had happened to me. I had brought no phone with me, so for all they knew, I could be dead.

The thought of them worrying had been a constant stress. Now they knew, and although they were clearly horrified, they didn't have to suffer the added fear of the unknown.

I couldn't have felt more grateful to River for the way she had comforted my mother when my mother had needed it most. I glanced back down at River's pretty face as we stepped back through the boundary. Her eyes were set forward in determination. I realized I had never known a girl as strong as her. Even my sister, for all her bravery… I honestly wasn't sure that she was capable of carrying herself with the same levelheadedness as River.

I didn't know exactly what had made River the way she was—I guessed it was rooted in her upbringing, and the difficult childhood she'd had— but at that moment, I didn't think it was possible for me to adore or respect a woman more.

Although Aisha, who'd brought us up to see my and River's parents, was still waiting for us within the boundary with a look of slight impatience on her face, I stopped River in her tracks. I slid an arm around her small waist and raised my other hand to support her head as I tilted it backward and kissed her deeply. No words from me were needed. I could see from the look in her eyes as I raised my head again that she understood what her gesture had meant to me.

Then I resumed my hold on her hand, and we closed the distance between us and Aisha. I could've sworn a scowl crossed the jinni's face on witnessing my display of affection for River, but it passed quickly. Aisha cleared her throat, flicking aside a lock of her curly black hair.

"Was there anything else you wanted?" she asked.

"Yes," I said. "But first let's return to your atrium." I'd already decided that I wanted to spend as little time as possible in the upper atrium to avoid bumping into Jeramiah, Michael, and other unsavory characters, so I had requested Nuriya to allot me an apartment down in the jinn's abode.

"As you wish," Aisha replied smoothly.

A thick mist appeared from nowhere and surrounded us, and the next second, we were standing in the Nasiris' gardens, a few feet away from the border of the sparkling swan-dotted lake.

"And now?" Aisha asked, raising a brow.

I paused, pulling my mind away from thoughts of River and my family and fixing it on my next move.

"I have a question," River said.

Aisha forced a smile. "What might that be?" she asked, the tone of her voice bordering on patronizing.

"All that time Ben and I were staying in The Oasis, how come you never made us aware of your presence? We had no idea that this place was inhabited by jinn—we thought it was just home to Jeramiah and his coven. Nobody would tell us why we'd been branded with these tattoos and who'd put them on us."

"Ah," Aisha said. "Well, half-blood, we deliberately keep ourselves hidden from new members… It can be quite overwhelming for them at first. Initially we tend to let them get used to their new life here and we try to make sure their stay is as comfortable as possible… then once we feel they're ready to be introduced to us—perhaps after a few weeks, sometimes a month or two, depending on the person—they are brought down to visit my aunt, Queen Nuri."

"So that's why you keep the entrance to your atrium well hidden?" River asked. "So new members don't come across it easily?"

"Precisely," Aisha said. "That—and also if there was ever a raid on this place, we would be the last to be found, and the last to be disturbed."

That last snippet of information caught my attention. "How could this place ever be raided?" I asked. "Isn't it under your protection?"

"Yes, of course," Aisha said quickly—a little too quickly. To my surprise, she looked a little flustered suddenly. "I just mean if a vampire happened to be careless and let a hunter capture and gain entrance with him, for example."

I eyed her curiously, not buying that explanation. The question played on my mind. *What being could ever be powerful enough to break in and raid a place protected by an ancient family of jinn?*

Aisha changed the subject. "It's about time for lunch. Why don't you join us? Queen Nuri will be there, and you'll get to meet the rest of my family too."

Lunch. The last thing I felt like doing was sitting down for lunch, but if this was going to be a family lunch with all the jinn present, perhaps River and I would glean some useful information. Besides, River might be hungry.

"Do you want to?" I asked her.

River paused, looking from Aisha to me. "Um… Okay," she replied.

Aisha looked relieved and forced another wide smile. "Splendid. Unfortunately, Ben only drinks human blood, but you, River, will adore the food. I promise you that it'll be quite unlike anything you've ever tasted before…"

"What do you jinn eat exactly?" River asked, looking rather unsettled.

"Oh, basically the same as humans… But my older sister, who loves to cook and usually plays chef of this place, really has a way with spices."

"Okay," River said, still appearing uncertain. "Thanks."

The jinni led us away from the gardens and toward the kitchen. As we drew near, I thought we were going to enter it, but instead, we passed right by it and she stopped us outside the next door along.

Aisha twisted the door handle and stepped inside. We followed after her, arriving in a grand circular dining hall. Right in the center was a long banquet table. It was immaculately set with golden plates and silver cutlery, and tall vases of irises decorated the center of the table.

Aisha gestured toward the chairs. "Well, take a seat wherever you want," she said. "Just don't sit at the head of the table. That spot is reserved for my aunt. We're a little early, but everyone else will be arriving soon. I'm going to see my sister in the kitchen. Wait here."

She vanished, leaving behind a veil of mist. River and I looked at each other, then back at the table. I pulled up a seat somewhere along the middle of it for River to sit down, and then took a seat next to her myself. River's eyes were wide and nervous as she took in the beauty of the room. I reached for her hand and planted a kiss on the back of it. Then we waited for the jinn to arrive.

We weren't waiting long. After perhaps five minutes, Aisha reappeared with another female jinni and a trolley loaded with steaming pots, jugs, and serving spoons.

"This is Safi, my sister," Aisha said. "Safi, this is Benjamin Novak and his half-blood."

I couldn't miss the way she didn't bother introducing River properly. I eyed Safi and was surprised by how much older she looked compared to Aisha.

Safi appeared quite uninterested in us. She glanced our way briefly before proceeding to place jugs of deep purple liquid on the table.

The door to the room creaked. I looked round to see more jinn had just entered the room. A lot more jinn. There must have been at least fifty of them. Nuriya and her lover Bahir were the only ones that I recognized, but most of them had similar features to Nuriya—except a handful with lighter hair, who apparently were members of the Nasiri family by marriage rather than blood. The jinn glanced at River and me already seated at the table, before making their way to their own chairs. I groaned internally as Aisha rushed to occupy the other seat next to me before someone else could take it.

Observing these strange creatures closely, I was surprised to see them sitting as if they had a backside. They looked perfectly normal while seated.

Nuriya gave River and me a warm smile.

"Good afternoon," she purred. She sat down at the head of the table.

I couldn't bring myself to smile back. The expression I returned looked like more of a grimace.

Once everyone was seated, Safi began making her way around the table with her trolley, delicately doling out portions of food onto each of the plates. She worked with surprising speed, and soon she had reached River. She began planting various preparations on River's plate—most of which I couldn't put a name to. There was a portion of steaming white rice, some kind of exotic-looking salad and a type of flatbread, but there was nothing else on her plate that I could recognize by either sight or smell.

Safi planted a generous jug of blood in front of me along with a tall glass. I looked at it, my mouth already watering. I didn't miss River eyeing it with disgust before she set her focus back on her own plate. I filled my glass to the brim.

Once everyone had been served, Nuriya stood up and gazed around the table. She held a crystal glass filled with that odd purple liquid, which, going by the smell, I assumed was some kind of juice rather than liquor.

"I'd like to introduce you all to Benjamin Novak and River Giovanni," she said smoothly. "I believe that this is the first time most of you are meeting them."

There were mutterings of, "Good afternoon."

"This really is quite a special lunch for all of us," she said. "It marks the day Benjamin Novak became a permanent member of our family. He has become eternally ours, and we eternally his."

Way to kill my appetite...

The rest of the jinn eyed me with a lot more curiosity after that little speech.

Nuriya sat down, and everyone began to dig into their food. For a while, I held off starting on my blood. I was too interested to see exactly how these creatures ate. But it turned out that there was really nothing interesting about it. I wasn't exactly sure how their bodies worked, having no visible lower half, but they appeared to consume food quite ordinarily, the way a human would.

I raised my glass to my lips and took a sip from the blood. That sweet, succulent blood. I still hadn't tasted anything like it. Jeramiah had told me it tasted so good because they kept the humans well, but I was interested in getting confirmation from the jinn.

"What is it about this blood?" I said, looking directly at Nuriya. "It's unlike any other I've tasted."

She raised a silk napkin to her mouth, daintily wiping her upper lip before responding. "We take good care of the humans upstairs," she replied, offering me another wide smile. "They're fed lots of fresh milk and other wholesome foods… As well as a homemade juice that my dear niece Safi here concocts herself."

My eyes set on Safi, who was still standing next to the trolley, watching with apparent pleasure as everyone tucked into her food.

"What's in the juice?" I asked.

"It's mostly plant-based," she replied, shortly.

I hadn't realized that diet could have such a drastic effect on the taste of human blood.

I looked down at River, who had begun chewing on the most recognizable substances on her plate— she had mixed the salad with the rice, and was eating it with the bread.

"How is it?" I asked in a low voice, as the other jinn began to chatter amongst themselves.

River's expression was conflicted as she chewed slowly and thoughtfully. "It's… delicious," she said.

"All you've touched is bread and rice salad!" Aisha's voice came from my right. Apparently she had been observing River and me closely. She raised her own plate to River and gestured toward a lumpy reddish preparation in the center of her plate. "You must try this next."

River eyed the dish cautiously. "What is this exactly?" River asked the jinni, indicating one of the lumps as she rolled it around on her plate.

"Stuffed and fried potato," Aisha answered.

"Stuffed with what?" River asked.

"That would be spoiling the surprise. Just try it, I promise you'll love it."

River looked reluctantly at the lump, then, scooping it up with a spoon, raised it to her mouth. Gingerly, she took a bite.

"Ouch!" River spat the lump out into her napkin and clutched the side of her jaw. "It's so hard! What the hell is that?"

Aisha giggled before proceeding to place one of her lumps in her mouth, then chew and swallow it with no problem at all.

River gaped at her. "How can you eat that?"

"Easy." After Aisha had finished swallowing, she bared her teeth, revealing how thick and sturdy they looked. Certainly not the jaws of a human.

"What was that?" River asked again.

It was Safi who answered: "Bone."

River glared at Aisha. "Why would you ask me to bite into that?"

Aisha just giggled in response.

"What kind of bone?" River asked.

"The only kind of bone we eat here," a female jinni on the other side of River replied. "Human bone, of course."

River's face drained of all color.

"Ground human bone is also in the salad dressing," Aisha added cheerfully. "That's what makes it so nice and thick."

River doubled over. The next thing I knew, she had vomited all over the floor.

I abandoned my glass of blood and bent down to help her up. But she gagged again and threw up a second time. Her knees were trembling. She wiped her mouth with the back of her hand, looking the jinn over with sheer disgust, the same way many of them were eyeing her after watching her vomit all over the dining room floor as they had lunch.

I'd hoped this luncheon would be an opportunity

to learn more about the jinn. Clearly, this hadn't been the brightest of ideas.

"Let's go," I muttered, picking River up. "Lunch is over."

Chapter 18: Ben

Neither River nor I bothered to apologize for her throwing up in the middle of the lunch. It was their damn fault for not warning River what she was eating.

Carrying River, I brought her back to the apartment that Nuriya had allotted to me. It was on the fifth floor, and while not nearly as large as the others, it was still infinitely more luxurious than the apartment I'd inhabited in the upper atrium.

I took her straight to the bathroom. She bent over

the seat and vomited some more, then washed her mouth out and downed gulps of water. I handed her a towel, which she wet and wiped her face with.

She still didn't look recovered.

"I need to take a shower."

"Okay," I said, backing out of the bathroom and heading to the room next door—my bedroom. I kept the door open so that she'd easily find me after she'd finished.

She entered the room about ten minutes later, wrapped in a bathrobe. Even now, she didn't look quite right. I led her to the kitchen and pointed to a bowl of fruit that had been set on the table.

"Dig into some of that," I said. "It will help take any aftertaste away."

She chose a ripe papaya, cut it in half, and began eating its flesh with a spoon.

I placed a glass of water next to her. She looked at me gratefully before downing the whole thing in a few gulps.

After she had finished the whole fruit, she slumped back in her chair. Although she was calmer, she still had a look of horror on her face.

"I can't believe I actually swallowed… some human." She shuddered. "God."

I looked at her grimly. "Welcome to my world."

She looked at me with newfound understanding in her eyes. She nodded, gulping, before changing the subject. "I guess now we know what Jeramiah must've been grinding."

"Yes," I said. "I suspect that's why they feed the humans so well. It's not to make their blood rich for the vampires. It's to make their bones strong and healthy."

"All that calcium in the camel milk," River muttered.

Our conversation trailed off. I sat with her in the kitchen until she showed signs of recovery. After ten minutes, she stood up.

"Okay," she said. "I need to get dressed. Is there anything I can change into in this apartment? My old clothes are disgusting by now."

We returned to my bedroom and I pulled open the tall closet. This was the first time that I'd looked inside, so I didn't know if there would be anything suitable. But, surprisingly, alongside men's clothing were shelves of women's clothing. River picked out the most comfortable-looking thing she could see—a light cotton dress—and I left the room while she changed.

Now that she had recovered, as much as I loathed to see Aisha again after the misery she had just caused River, thanks to Nuriya delegating my wishes to her, I had no choice.

Once we left the apartment, we didn't have to travel far before I spotted her. Apparently the jinn had finished lunch by now and were leaving the dining hall. I sped up, reaching Aisha before she could turn down a staircase.

"We need to talk," I said.

She turned around, and as her eyes fell to River, there was an infuriating smirk on her face. Then her expression turned to mock apology.

"Listen," she said to River, "I'm sorry. You're half vampire. I didn't know that you'd have such a reaction to tasting a bit of human…"

"I have another wish that you need to grant," I said, not wanting her to rub the traumatic experience in for River even more. "And this one carries a lot more weight than what I've asked of you so far. I suspect that you're going to have to take me to Nuriya to have it fulfilled."

"What is it?" she asked, planting her hands on her hips.

"I need you to get rid of the bloodlust I have for humans."

"Why do you want to do that?"

"Can you do it or not?" I asked, unwilling to indulge her in even a single unnecessary question.

"Well, what do you mean exactly? You want to become a human? I can't see how else you would stop craving human blood. As a vampire, it's just ingrained in your nature to want it."

"I want you to make me a human, and then I want to turn into a half-blood. But just so you are aware," I continued, "I already tried to turn back into a human. I don't know if you know of the cure to vampirism that was discovered eighteen years ago. It involves consuming the blood of an immune and then being exposed to the sun for several hours. I took that same cure that had worked for countless vampires before me, but it failed to turn me back."

Aisha looked a little lost. "I... I don't have experience with this kind of thing. Something like this... you're asking me to permanently alter your very identity..." She paused. "I'm going to have to talk to my aunt about this."

As I suspected...

My eyes shot toward the entrance of the dining hall. It was my good luck that Nuriya was exiting just as we stood here. Aisha called to her and beckoned her over.

Nuriya first looked at River. The queen had a genuine look of apology and regret on her face. "I am very sorry for what happened," she said, clasping her hands around River's shoulders. "How are you feeling?"

River nodded stiffly.

Then I repeated what I wanted to the queen. After I'd finished explaining, she didn't respond for several moments. She just remained quiet, eyeing me closely.

"Benjamin," she said finally. "There is a lot we jinn can do—we can work magic and miracles, and we can influence the mind unlike almost any other creature that exists—but what you are asking is for us to alter the very fabric of your being."

"'Fabric of my being'? What are you talking about?" I asked, alarm and frustration taking hold of me. I'd just sold myself to these creatures with the belief that they could solve any problem I had. "I was born a human. If anything, *that* is the fabric of my being. That is my true identity."

Nuriya shook her head slowly. "You are different, Benjamin…"

"Why don't you just try?" River butted in, clearly sensing my temper.

"My dear," the jinni replied, "as much as I can help Benjamin in a thousand different ways, I am, after all, not God."

I swore beneath my breath.

Great. That's just great.

"But Ben and I have already seen that you can

transform people and change their identities," River continued. "We saw you turn our witches into birds!"

"That was an entirely different scenario, my dear," she said, shaking her head again. "There's much about Benjamin that you don't know."

"So you do know what is wrong with me at least, don't you?" I said, trying to reel in my frustration. "Those weeks that I was away from The Oasis, I heard your voice in my head, telling me that you knew who I was and knew what I wanted. Then you gave me that vision of myself as an infant."

To my relief, Nuriya nodded. "Yes, indeed."

"So if you're telling me that you can't turn me back into a human, and you're not willing to even try, then at least you can explain the vision that I had. You can tell me why I am like this, and what happened. Who was that Hawk exactly? Where did she take me?"

Nuriya's face lit up. "Of course, we can tell you everything that happened in your past. Aisha is fully capable of doing that. Aren't you?"

Aisha nodded enthusiastically. "Oh, yes."

"Then I will leave you with her, my son…"

"No! Wait—"

Brushing a hand against my cheek, Nuriya vanished in a puff of smoke.

I stamped my foot in frustration. I'd been about to insist that the queen at least grant me my wish rather than the insufferable Aisha. The damn jinni had given me no chance.

Infuriating woman.

"So now we know what we're doing," Aisha said briskly, clasping her hands together and setting her focus back on me. "But before I take you back in time and give you more visions, I suggest you take some time out."

"What?"

"The visions I'm about to impart on you will be a lot to take in. You've had a stressful past twenty-four hours. Your mind needs to rest and unwind. Relaxation will help it to open up."

I brushed her aside. "Forget that. Just give me the visions now."

"Benjamin, I must insist on this. If you don't, you

won't have a clear mind, and you won't be able to retain all the information you desire."

River squeezed my hand. "Maybe you should do as she suggests," she said quietly.

I breathed out sharply. "Okay. I'll return to my apartment and sit in a chair for fifteen minutes."

"No, no, no," Aisha said, looking amused. "You need at the very least one hour, and sitting in a chair is no way to unwind. *I* will show you exactly how you must do this..."

Not waiting for my approval, the jinni transported River and me to a softly lit chamber filled with a light blue mist and a heady aroma of frankincense.

There were six round steaming pools that looked like a cross between jacuzzis and hot tubs. The stone walls were a warm earthy color, as were the floors, giving the whole place a rustic feel.

"Relax in one of these baths for an hour," Aisha said.

In the few moments I'd been in the room, breathing in the exotic-smelling incense, I could already feel my head becoming lighter.

"There is a changing room over there," Aisha continued, pointing to the far corner of the room. "You'll find everything you need in there." Then she addressed River. "If you're staying here with him too, the women's changing room is on the opposite side."

I looked up at a large clock that was fixed near the ceiling, noting the time. "I'll stay here for sixty minutes," I told the jinni, "and not a moment longer."

"All right," Aisha said. "And by the way, when you need to summon me, you don't have to come looking for me. You have your amulet." She gestured toward the gold band around my wrist. "All you need to do is brush the snake's head."

"Okay…" I said, eyeing the band. Aisha gave River and me one last look before taking her leave.

I headed toward the men's changing room, while River headed to the women's.

The men's was a ridiculously large room for a changing room—and lavishly decorated, as with the rest of this place. The floor and walls were made of marble, and the embroidered towels were the softest

I'd ever touched in my life. I found a stack of crisp folded swimshorts. I took a pair and slipped them on. Heading back into the spa, I was surprised to see River already waiting for me. My breath hitched as I took in how stunning she looked in a thin red bikini. She had bunched her long, rich brown hair over one shoulder, and this was the first time I'd seen so much of her curves. I found myself slightly speechless.

"Uh, shall we?" I pointed to the nearest bath to us and we both slipped inside.

The water was warm and fragrant as it bubbled against my body. We sat opposite each other against the walls of the pool. Then River left her spot and glided toward me. At first she moved slowly, timidly, but when she reached me, her hands gripped my arms and she pulled herself onto my lap. Her chest pressing against mine, she moved in to kiss me. As her luscious lips were a split second from touching mine, a voice called from the women's changing room.

"You said something, Ben?"

It was River's voice.

I looked in confusion toward the door of the changing room. Then back at the girl sitting on top of me. I swore. Inches away from my face was no longer the vision of River, but the gleaming face of Aisha.

She burst out laughing hysterically. Then, before I could grab her neck, she vanished.

Curse that girl!

The real River stepped out of the changing room, in the same thin red bikini, and looking just as breathtaking.

"You said something?" she repeated, moving toward my pool.

As she slid into the water and took a seat next to me, I told her what just happened. She flinched slightly as I described how Aisha had come on to me.

"She was going to kiss you?" River said, an unmistakable hint of jealousy in her voice.

"She would have," I said, "if I hadn't heard your voice calling from the changing room."

River caught my arms, the same way Aisha had done. She sat on my knees, facing me.

"She sat on you like this?" she asked.

A slight smile curved the corners of my lips. I could already see where she was going with this. I placed my hands on River's hips, sliding her down my knees until she was sitting on my thighs.

"Like this," I replied. "But how do I know it's you this time?" I dropped my voice to a whisper.

She closed the distance between our faces and kissed my lips. When she drew away, she had a cheeky smile on her face.

"Do you think anyone else could kiss you like that?"

I paused, feigning thought. "I'd need you to do it again for me to be sure..." I ran my hands up her back before closing my lips around hers, more slowly this time, and more deeply. I didn't give her my answer for another five minutes. I got too lost in her, her soft tongue, her full lips, the contours of her body melding with mine as we held each other so closely.

No. I doubted there was a woman in the world who could make me feel the way River did.

She drew away from me in the water, her lips

flushed red and slightly swollen. She cocked her head to one side. "Well?"

"Hmm… I *think* you're River."

She grinned, nudging me in the shoulder. She submerged herself in the water and reappeared, her hair slicked back. Her bikini clung to her chest, pearls of water dripping from her hair and eyelashes, making trails down the shape of her body. Damn. River looked beautiful in water.

I couldn't keep myself from joining her in the center of the pool. I placed my hands on her thighs, drawing her toward me again. I guided her into wrapping her legs around my waist. She placed her hands on top of my head.

"Come down with me," she said.

I dipped the two of us underwater. Her mouth pressed against mine. I'd never made out underwater before, and it was an odd experience. But making out with River was something I'd relish anytime and anywhere.

"You're beautiful," I said, as I lifted her up again.

She rested her forehead against mine, staring so

closely into my eyes that I lost focus. "So are you," she whispered. "Prince Benjamin." A playful smile crossed her lips. "If we got married one day, would that make me a princess?"

I chuckled, unable to keep myself from responding with: "You don't need me to be a princess."

She giggled. "You're so cheesy."

She ran her hands through my hair. I wasn't quite sure what she was doing with it—it felt like she was trying to make it spike upwards. Apparently failing in her endeavor, she cast her eyes around the chamber. Her face lit up. She pointed toward what appeared to be four massage tables lined up along one of the walls.

"Aisha said that you need to wind down, right?"

"You're winding me down just fine..."

"Well, I have another idea," she said.

She detached herself from me and climbed out of the pool. I admired her graceful form as she walked across the room. She bent down when she reached the massage tables and removed three bottles from a little cabinet next to them. She returned to me and set the bottles down in a row at the side of the pool.

"Move to the steps," she said.

I did as she'd requested, and sat down on one of the steps, my back facing her. She picked up the first bottle. When she opened it, the scent that drifted out was divine. Planting her feet either side of me, she sat behind me, one step higher, and started to massage the back of my neck with the oil. Her hands, wonderfully firm, kneaded against my muscles, releasing tension I hadn't even realized I'd had. I was surprised by how good she was.

"Did someone teach you?" I asked.

"In another life, my mom was a sports injury therapist," River replied. "She studied massage, and I learnt a few tips from her."

She massaged me for the next ten minutes, and I was sure she would've continued for the rest of the hour if I hadn't caught her hands and stopped her.

"Okay," I said, raising myself from the step, and guiding her to sit in my place. "Now it's your turn."

Pouring some oil into my hand, I began massaging her back. I doubted I was doing as good of a job as she had with me, but she seemed to be enjoying it thoroughly. She closed her eyes, her head lolling back slightly as I worked my way around her shoulder blades. Every so often, I leaned in to kiss the side of her neck or the backs of her shoulders. I relished the slight tremor that ran through her body each time my lips grazed her.

When we were done, we both slipped back down into the pool to rinse off the oil.

Then I looked up at the clock. "Just five more minutes until an hour is gone," I said. "Any final requests?"

"Final requests," she said thoughtfully. "Hmm... Could you wish for Aisha to banish herself from The Oasis?"

River was joking, but there was a part of me that actually considered requesting that of Nuriya. Unfortunately, I guessed that that would be another thing that was off boundaries—requesting punishment or harm to be done to a member of her own family.

After indulging myself in another round of River's

sweet kisses, I led her out of the pool where we split to get dried and changed.

I found a clean pair of clothes to wear—a loose shirt and pants—and, not bothering to dry my hair, I left the changing room to find Aisha already hovering by one of the pools. I was disappointed that she was here already because I'd been hoping that I could practice summoning her with the snake band.

If it hadn't been for the hour of bliss I had just spent with River, I would've let loose my anger at what she'd almost tricked me into doing. But I was feeling too relaxed and content to want to drag my mind there, so I let it go.

"You're certainly looking more relaxed now," Aisha said, eyeing me from head to foot, a glint of amusement in her gaze.

"Thanks to my girlfriend," I said.

That seemed to sour the jinni's mood. She pursed her lips, and paused for a moment before saying, "So are you ready for the visions now?"

"One moment," I said, walking toward the women's changing room. I stood outside the door and was about to ask River how much longer she'd be when she stepped out. She wore the same cotton dress she had taken from my bedroom and had tied her damp hair up in a bun.

We walked back to Aisha.

"Yes," I said to the jinni. "I'm ready."

"River shouldn't be with you for this," Aisha said.

The calmness River had managed to induce me into stirred.

Whatever crush this jinni had on me was turning into a serious problem. It was becoming clear that she was barely able to have a single interaction without her bias against River coming into play in one way or another.

I took a deep breath, trying to maintain my calm.

"River stays with me," I said steadily. "I'm not letting her out of my sight while she's in this place."

"I'm serious, Benjamin," Aisha said. "Another person in the room, other than you and me, will simply be a distraction."

"River was lying with me in the same bed when I had the vision of myself as an infant," I shot back. "I assimilated the information in that vision just fine."

"But you don't know how much more you might have gleaned had you been by yourself," Aisha said, crossing her arms over her chest.

River heaved a sigh. "Look, Ben," she said, tugging on my hand for me to face her. "It's not a big deal. I'll just... hang around until you're done. If there's even a chance—"

I shook my head. "No," I said, "I don't—"

River placed her hands on my shoulders. "If there's even a chance that Aisha is right, I should sit out of this. I'll be fine. You already made clear that I'm not to be harmed."

"Oh, yes," Aisha said, butting in as usual. "You don't need to worry about River. She will be perfectly safe. Besides, if you're really worried, I can take her to wait in Queen Nuri's quarters. Nobody would dare do anything to her there. I'll take her to the same room where her brother was staying."

I paused, clenching my jaw. "How long is this going to take?" I asked. "How much do you really have to show me?"

"I suspect we will be an hour or two," Aisha said.

"That's not long at all," River said, trying to reassure me.

"All right," I said. "But Aisha, I'm coming with you to drop River off at Nuri's place." *I need to be sure that's indeed where you plan to take her...*

"Of course," Aisha said. "We'll go there now together."

The spa vanished and we reappeared in the same stately bedroom where River had been taken to meet her cured brother. River moved toward the bed and sat down on the edge of it. She offered me a warm smile. "I'll be fine," she said. "Just go now."

I walked over to her and kissed her cheek. Still aching with the thought of leaving her, I stepped away to allow Aisha to transport me to wherever it was she planned to reveal the missing pieces of my past.

CHAPTER 19: RIVER

After Ben left the room with Aisha, I leaned back on the bed. A smile formed on my lips as I recalled the hour of sheer bliss I'd just spent with Ben. *Benjamin Novak. My boyfriend.* The word sent tingles down my spine. I'd never had a boyfriend, and the idea that someone as gorgeous as Ben could be my first... I felt like the luckiest girl in the world.

I played back every detail of our time in that spa, every lingering kiss, every slow caress, every flirtatious comment... I felt breathless as I relived it all again.

That hour I'd just spent with the vampire had lifted my heart to such a height, it was hard to believe that it would ever come down again.

The heat he sparked in me just from his mere touch, it was unlike anything I'd experienced in my life. It felt like I could never be satiated by his company. I just wanted him, all of him, all the time.

The thought of Aisha trying to kiss him made my heart burn. I hadn't considered myself the jealous type, so I was surprised by how strongly my emotions had tugged at me. It was just further confirmation how much Ben had come to mean to me.

Aisha.

I wasn't sure if that jinni had been telling the truth about it being better for Ben to be alone while she imparted visions to him, but I'd thought that it was better not to risk being there. I didn't feel afraid, because Ben had already wished for my safety while staying here. And besides, it was just an hour or two.

I just hoped that Aisha wouldn't try anything else now she had Ben alone. He hated her guts, but I didn't trust anything about that jinni. Ben and I still weren't fully aware of what powers they possessed. I didn't know just how far they stretched over influencing a person.

Still, I comforted myself, it was only a couple of hours.

I prayed that during this time, Benjamin would finally find the answers he'd been looking for. Even though we still had no idea how we would get him free from this bond he'd formed with the jinn, at least he could get rid of his bloodlust.

Ever since I met him I'd watched him drink human blood—heck, I'd even witnessed him slaughter humans and drink from their throats. I had been amply acquainted with the idea of supernaturals using humans for food—but absolutely nothing could have prepared me for the feeling of eating human myself. Human bone at that. I shivered. I still hadn't recovered from it.

The cooing of a bird interrupted my thoughts. I looked toward the ornamental cage near the side of the bed, my eyes fixing on the same white dove I'd seen in here earlier. I wasn't sure whether it was male or female, but it was clear that it was miserable. It kept beating its wings against the sides of the cage, as if trying to get out. I lifted myself off the bed and moved toward it, peering through the bars. *Poor thing.* I'd always thought that keeping birds as pets was cruel.

Its feet clinging to the edges of the cage, it continued to flap. I stuck a finger through the bars. I wasn't even sure why I did it. I wanted to just comfort it in some way, and I figured that touch would be the best way to do that. I was surprised when it didn't shy away as I stroked its head. Rather, it seemed to draw comfort from me.

"There, there," I said softly. "I'm not going to hurt you."

There were lots of birds in the spacious gardens outside who were allowed to fly around freely. It didn't seem fair that this beautiful dove should be trapped in here.

I scanned the room, as if a jinni might read my thoughts and appear to scold me.

Then I set my focus on the cage. I eyed it over,

trying to figure out if there was any way to open it. Unfortunately, the door was locked. There was a tiny keyhole. Leaving the cage, I looked around the room for a key. I looked on the mantelpiece, on shelves, inside drawers, in the closet… but didn't find anything. Walking back to the cage, I gripped its door and pulled. It didn't seem to be very steady at all, and I was strong. It wouldn't take much for me to just force it open.

It seemed that the dove was just being kept as an ornament in this spare room. I couldn't believe Nuriya would be too furious if I let it free in the gardens. Besides, even if she got mad, Ben could just wish for her to forgive me…

As quietly as I could, I pried open the door and reached inside the cage. I was afraid that the dove might immediately try to fly out of reach. So before it could escape, I closed my hands around it, trying to tuck back its wings gently and stop it from flapping so much. To my surprise, it became strangely calm as I touched it. It didn't put up any fight as I folded back its wings. I lifted it out of the cage and, sitting back down on the bed, placed it on my lap and began to stroke it. As I looked at it more closely, it appeared that this was a female.

I stroked her for about a minute, even though she seemed calm enough, because I wanted her to get used to me before I carried her out of the room. Then, standing up from the bed, I wrapped her in the folds of my dress before stepping out into the corridor. I moved through the apartment, hoping that I wouldn't bump into anyone. It was quiet, and I couldn't sense anyone nearby, but jinn had the ability to show up when they were least expected. I made it to the front door without passing anyone, the dove still sitting calmly in my hands as I kept her covered. I opened the front door as quietly as I could and then stepped outside onto the veranda. I moved to the edge of it and looked down toward the sprawling gardens. Flocks of birds flew from tree to tree, chirping. Looking all around me to check that nobody was watching, I lifted the fabric of my dress and removed my hands from her wings, allowing her to fly free.

"Go on," I whispered.

I'd expected her to immediately spread her wings and go shooting toward freedom in the gardens. But she did nothing of the sort. If anything, her feet tightened around my forefinger, as though she was afraid to fly.

Looking anxiously around again to check that nobody was coming our way, I tried to give her a little nudge with my other hand.

"Go on," I whispered. "Go make some friends."

Still, she remained clinging to me. I tried to unclasp her feet from my finger, but as I did, she just shuffled along and instead clasped them around my thumb.

What is it with this bird?

Either she had really taken a liking to me, or she had been raised her whole life in that cage and freedom scared her. Perhaps she needed me to take her down to the gardens, let her walk around on the grass a bit, get used to the surroundings before she would feel more comfortable about flying free.

I was about to do just that when I turned around

to find myself face to face with a vampire I hoped I'd never have to see again.

Michael Gallow.

His brown eyes registered as much surprise to see me as I felt to see him. Then his expression turned cold.

A part of me wanted to bolt, not to even be within a mile of this man, but another part of me didn't want to show fear or weakness before him. So I stood my ground.

He eyed the bird briefly before raising his eyes to my face again. He looked like he was about to open his mouth and say something, but instead, he just clenched his jaw harder and, turning on his heel, walked away without a word. My eyes followed him as he walked away along the veranda toward the kitchen and disappeared through the door. I assumed he was returning to the upper atrium.

Good riddance.

I wondered what he'd been doing down here. From the look on his face, it was clear that the jinn hadn't informed him that we had returned—I wondered if they had informed Jeramiah. I knew Ben didn't want Jeramiah knowing that we had returned here, but now that Michael knew, I was sure that it was only a matter of time before Ben's cousin found out.

Tearing my thoughts away from the vampire, I continued on my way down to the gardens. I walked through several exquisite flower gardens and stopped when I reached the bank of the glistening lake. I sat down on the soft grass and placed the dove in front of me. Still her feet clung to me, but I managed to detach her from my hand. I remained kneeling so that I would be next to her and she wouldn't feel like I was leaving, and hoped that she would explore a little on her own two feet. But she didn't. She didn't even seem to look around at all. She just remained facing me, and the moment she got the chance, she jumped back into my hands.

I heaved a sigh.

I couldn't bring myself to carry her back into Nuriya's apartment and put her in the cage again. Besides, this made no sense. She had looked so desperate to get out of the cage before, the way she had been flapping against those bars.

So I tried more tactics for the next hour. I took her on a tour around the lush gardens, and even tried to place her on a tree, but the dove ended up flying back to me and planting herself on my shoulder.

"You really like me, don't you," I muttered.

In the end, I gave up. No matter how much I tried, there was no convincing this dove that the gardens would be a better home for her than my hands. So I saw no choice but to return with her to Nuriya's quarters.

She had her chance…

I guess at least I've got a friend now to keep me company until Ben's finished with Aisha. Or rather, until she's finished with him…

The bird fluttered from my hand and perched on my forearm while I made our way out of the gardens and back up to Nuriya's quarters. On my way down, I had left the door to her apartment slightly ajar, and I was pleased to see that it had remained so. I didn't have to knock and draw someone's attention. I clicked the door shut behind me, and, cupping the dove in my hands and covering her again with my dress, I hurried back to the spare room and locked us inside.

I looked around, wondering what I was going to do to occupy myself for the next hour while I waited for Ben to finish. I set the dove on my shoulder and then walked around the room, examining the shelves and looking for something to read. I didn't find any books at all in here, but I did find a pad of paper along with an old-fashioned quill and ink pot on a desk in one corner of the room. I sat down, tore off a sheet from the pad, and dipped the quill in the ink. I'd never been much of an artist, but I needed something to distract my mind from looking up at the clock every few minutes and wondering how things were going with Ben.

I decided to see if I could draw one of the jinn. My attempt was cut short, however, as the dove flew at the pot of ink and knocked it off the desk.

Damn!

The white floor was splattered with dark blue ink.

I grabbed some tissues from the ensuite bathroom and motioned to start cleaning up when again, the dove did something strange. She flew down directly in front of the mess and spread her wings, as if trying to form a barrier between me and the ink. I withdrew my hand and stood up, staring down in confusion at the bird.

What has gotten into this creature's head?

She stepped right into a thick blot of ink, completely soaking her feet in the substance, and then flew to a patch of floor that had remained untouched by the breakage.

The bird landed and began walking slowly… in a curve, leaving behind her a trail of ink. As soon as she had formed a half circle, she flew up again, and then landed again about half a foot away. She began walking again in a curve—though this time coming full circle. Then she lifted herself into the air and landed a short distance away for a third time. Her movement this time seemed odd. She walked in a straight line, then curved in a half circle, before walking diagonally again in a straight line leaving behind… the letter R?

Any thought that this could just be some wild coincidence soon vanished from my head as the dove finished her trail. I found myself staring down at the word:

CORRINE.

Oh, God.

I've found her.

Chapter 20: Ben

Aisha ended up transporting me to a small dim room. At first, I wondered whether we were even still within the jinn's atrium. The room seemed so bare and unremarkable compared to the rest of their underground palace. I even insisted that I step out of the door and ensure that she hadn't taken me somewhere else. But she was telling the truth. We were still within the atrium.

We were on the ground level, in what appeared to be some kind of storage room. She'd placed two comfortable armchairs in there, but other than that, the room was totally empty.

"We just needed as plain a room as possible," Aisha explained. "No distractions. I will even turn out the lights once we start."

Turn out the lights. I didn't like the sound of being alone in a pitch-black room with Aisha. Although I could see in the dark, the lack of lighting might give her a false sense of security and I didn't know what tricks she might try. Still, I had to get this done. She held the answers I needed.

"Take a seat," Aisha said, as she closed the door.

I sat down, gripping the arms of the chair, and leaned back.

"Make sure you're comfortable and feeling relaxed," she said, her voice soft and alarmingly close to my ear. She had moved right behind me.

Then her hands slipped onto my shoulders. She attempted to massage me, but I shoved off her hands before she could start.

I glared daggers at her. "I'm relaxed," I said curtly. "Now let's get on with it."

She pouted, then moved over to the second chair, though she did not sit down. She remained hovering directly in front of me.

"Close your eyes then," she said.

Again, I felt uncomfortable about closing my eyes with her in the room. But at least for now, she seemed to be staying put where she was.

So I closed my eyes and leaned further back in the chair. And almost as soon as I did, a vision took hold of my mind…

A tall, lean figure covered in a cloak traveled along a rocky beach in the dead of night. It was a man, from the broadness of his shoulders and the strength of his walk. He carried a bundle in his arms—an infant, wrapped in a blanket.

The moon was the only light to guide him as he weaved in and out of the rocks. He stopped at the foot of a cliff that bordered the rocky shore. Heavy wings shot out from beneath his cloak. He flew upward, higher and higher, until he landed on a ledge about halfway up the cliff. Now he stood before a narrow crevice.

Folding his wings, he stepped sideways and moved

into it. He reappeared in a dark, damp tunnel, completely shut off from the rays of the moon. Still, the figure seemed to find his way as he moved forward. He wound his way round the tunnel, careful to keep the infant's fragile body sheltered from any protruding rocks in the walls, and finally arrived outside an old oak door. The wood was rotting from dampness and age, the iron handle rusting. He gripped the handle and tried to open it, but it was locked fast. He took one step back, and, holding the baby in one arm only, used his right hand to bang against the door.

His deep voice boomed out. "Hortencia! I know you are in here."

The dripping of water from stalactites and the distant thundering of waves outside the tunnel were the only sounds to be heard.

"Hortencia!" the man called again after several moments. "It is I, Arron of Aviary. Grant me entrance now, or I will break down your door."

Footsteps sounded, softly at first, then growing louder as they approached the other side of the door. The door handle rattled as someone on the other side clasped it.

"You're not welcome here," a quiet female voice

responded.

"You heard me," Arron replied. "Open the door."

There was a pause, and then came the clinking of keys. Metal scratched against metal, and then there was the sound of a bolt being drawn. Then the door groaned open, sending echoes off the walls of the tunnel.

Standing before the man was a small woman with a round, heart-shaped face and almost no hair. Her skin etched with circular black symbols and she wore a dark green robe. A strange silver visor covered her eyes, and the parts of her youthful face that were visible bore piercings.

"How did you find me?" she asked, her lip curling.

"The information came out of a particularly grueling session of torture with your aunt. We have her in Aviary, and she won't be let free until I have your counsel."

The woman grimaced. It was hard to tell how much of her distaste came from hearing that her aunt had been kidnapped, and how much from the fact that Arron had found her place and disturbed her.

"Let's be done with it," the woman said.

"Hold out your arms," Arron said. He shifted the baby from his arms into the woman's.

A small gasp escaped her lips the moment she touched the infant. Although she remained looking straight ahead, toward the direction of Arron's voice, and not down at the child.

Arron continued, "Through your blindness, what do you see?"

Her legs seemed suddenly weak, and she staggered back, her back hitting the oak door. Her black tattoos began to swirl and move, migrating around her skin.

"The child of an immune... and a former vampire. Derek Novak, no less."

"He was brought to us by a rogue vampire, Kiev Novalic. What do you advise that we do with the infant? How can he be valuable to us in our war against the Elders?"

The woman paused, chewing on her lower lip. She swayed a little on her feet. Her hands loosened around the infant, then tightened again. Her tattoos stopped moving.

Then she uttered only six words in response:

"Keep him away from the Elders."

The scene faded, giving way immediately to

another.

Holding the infant, Arron stood on a shady veranda sheltered by towering treetops. The Hawk lowered the infant into a cradle in the center of the platform and covered the crib with a light silk cloth. He walked several feet away toward the entrance of a grand wooden structure—a lavish treehouse residence—and stepped inside. Standing in the entrance room, in the middle of the shiny wooden floor, was a familiar female Hawk with curly auburn hair and a black beak.

She looked steadily at Arron. He closed the distance between them, and, holding her hands, locked beaks with her in what one could only assume was a kiss.

"How did it go?" the woman asked, her voice smooth and gentle. "Did you find the oracle?"

"Yes, my love," Arron replied, taking her hand and pulling her into a living room. They both sat down in soft cushioned chairs. "The boy is as I thought... a potential threat to us, yet also a bargaining tool if things don't go according to plan. The oracle's advice was that we must keep him safe in Aviary at all costs."

The woman's gaze seemed oddly distant as she

nodded. "Yes, Arron. We must."

My eyes shot open in the dark chamber. Aisha was still standing in the same spot.

My mind reeled from what I had just seen, as I tried to make sense of it all. That female Hawk… she was the same one I'd seen in the very first vision—the same one who'd brought me to Cruor. Yet she seemed to be Arron's wife, or lover? Why would she betray her own man? Heck, her own people? And who was Hortencia, that oracle woman, exactly? I considered asking one of the hundred questions flooding my brain, but I was too anxious to see more.

"Continue," I said.

Aisha bowed courteously. "Your wish is my command," she said with a grin.

I closed my eyes, allowing my mind to be hijacked once again.

The vision unfolded in the same living room of Arron's treehouse residence. The infant's cradle had been brought inside the room, and a young blonde girl sat near it on a couch, holding the baby in her arms and nursing him with a bottle.

Arron stepped into the room, accompanied by another female Hawk—a different woman to the one he'd sat with earlier in this very room. Both of them had tense expressions on their faces as they held hands.

"Jada," Arron addressed the young girl. "Carry the baby to the dining room and keep watch for my wife while you care for him. She's not due back for another two hours, but just in case... Warn me." His eyes were sharp as they dug into her.

"A-All right," Jada replied. Gathering up the baby, she hurried out of the room.

Arron clutched the hand of the female Hawk and led her out of the room. They headed upstairs, and, reaching a landing, Arron pulled her toward a bedroom.

"We shouldn't be doing this," the woman whispered, stopping in the doorway.

Arron looked at her intensely. "War is upon us. If not now, then when?"

The woman relented. She stepped toward Arron, who grabbed her waist, and then locked the door behind them.

The vision withdrew from the house and shifted to give a bird's eye view of the treehouse residence. Perched in a tree parallel to the bedroom Arron and his mistress had retreated into was the dark figure of a Hawk. She wore a black cloak with the hood pulled up. A stray lock of curly auburn hair revealed this Hawk's identity. Her eyes were fixed on the drawn blinds of the bedroom window. From the look on her face, she already knew exactly what was going on in there.

Her eyes were fiery, her fists clenched. After watching the window for several more minutes, her wings shot open and she swept herself away from the tree in a rage.

The treetop residence vanished, and another scene immediately took its place. It was nighttime and the same female Hawk—Arron's wife—stood alone on a rocky beach that was lined with jungle. Her wild red hair splayed in the wind as she stared out toward the rough waves. There appeared to be no sorrow in her eyes, only fury.

Stones crunched. She looked to her right, further up along the shore. A lone man had appeared. The Hawk moved toward him. Wearing a deep red robe, he was tall and wiry, with small gray eyes and skin so pale there was no mistaking him for anything but a bloodsucker. And yet there was something odd about his appearance. His features were lopsided. His mouth hung a little in one corner, and one of his eyelids was half closed. It was possible to make out a slight yellow tinge on certain areas of his skin—around the throat, his right wrist, and on the tips of his fingers.

"Nelda," he said in a gravelly voice.

The Hawk bowed her head slightly.

"Whatever you called me out here for, it had better be good."

"It is," the Hawk replied, her voice surprisingly steady. "Trust me, you won't regret this visit."

The man looked around, almost as though he was worried that it was a trap.

"Then tell me," he said. "This vessel I'm inhabiting is weakening, and it must be strong enough for me to travel back in. I don't have long."

"I am no longer loyal to my husband," Nelda began.

The vampire let out a scoff. "When were you ever loyal to him?"

The Hawk shot a glare at him. "Before he thought he could play me for a fool." She took a deep breath, *apparently trying to reel in her temper. "I plan to leave him, and indeed leave Aviary, before your army storms the place. I've had enough of this life and these people whom I barely even consider my own anymore... But before I leave, I need to do something that'll make Arron regret ever having betrayed me."*

The vampire had a look of disbelief on his face, but Nelda continued regardless. "The truth is," she said, "I have been tired of Arron and his rule here for some time now—the sheer hypocrisy of his methods. But there was a part of me that still loved him. And that is why I hung on all this time. Otherwise I would have left and become a wanderer many years ago. Now, I suppose that I should be grateful to him for making it easy for me to break away. I have no qualms about leaving him anymore... but before I do, it's only fair that I give him a taste of what betrayal feels like..." Her jaw tensed. "I want to see him and his whole damn kingdom come crashing down."

It looked as though the vampire was trying to raise a brow, but instead it twitched before collapsing.

Nelda took a deep breath. "That's where you come in," she continued. "I-I have something that could be of… *great value to you in your attack against Aviary. Something that could possibly be the difference between winning and losing."*

"What is it?" the vampire asked, taking a step closer.

"A male infant who is capable of being imprinted upon."

The vampire froze. "Where is this child? How do you know that he could be imprinted upon?"

"He is within Aviary. My husband went to visit an oracle… Hortencia. She gave him advice as to what to do with the child. I returned to see her without him and received answers of my own."

She paused, eyeing the vampire closely, as if gauging his interest and wanting him to prompt her to continue—which he did.

"Go on."

"Hortencia saw in the boy a great potential for use by the Elders, and that is why she instructed my husband to keep the boy with us. The baby is currently under Arron's wing… almost literally. He keeps the baby close to him much of the time, sometimes even during meetings, though the infant occasionally visits the medical building. In either case, I have easy access to

him."

The vampire held up a hand and narrowed his eyes. "Tell me, Nelda. Why should I believe a word you're saying?"

"I have been truthful about my motives," Nelda replied. "But you don't have to believe me, because I am asking for nothing in return. I'm offering you up the baby. Your acceptance of him is the only payment I require."

The vampire crossed his arms over his chest. "Tell me more about what the oracle said."

"She sees that this conflict is not one either side can take lightly. She doesn't see a positive outcome for anyone. However, there is something you can do to gain a significant advantage... Since the baby I speak of is a product of Derek Novak, formerly a vampire, and his immune wife, the possibilities are far, far greater than just an ordinary human. As I said, you can imprint on him—that is, infect him with your nature—and it will lie dormant within the baby. He will appear just like an ordinary human infant, and Arron won't have a clue what happened."

"And you would be willing to deliver the child

directly to Cruor?" the vampire asked.

"Yes. Directly to your leader. Then after the Elder has done the deed, I would return the baby to his crib in Arron's quarters, and there he would remain... until the time approached for you to storm the place. Having already infected him, one of you—perhaps even your leader himself—could inhabit him as a vessel, the way you would a fully-turned vampire. Since he is situated within Aviary's inner city, I'm sure you realize how valuable this could be..."

The vampire's eyes glinted.

"Very well... Bring the child to us."

I was panting as I opened my eyes. Aisha, still hovering in the same position, was looking down at me calmly. I shot up from my seat and clutched my head as the final traces of the vision evaporated from my mind.

Despite the revelations I'd just been given, I still felt utterly confused.

"When I was taken to Cruor by that redheaded Hawk, Arron's wife," I began, trying to organize my jumbled mind, "in that very first vision that you gave me… that presence that engulfed me, that was one of the Elders' leaders?"

"That's right," Aisha replied. "One of the strongest of their kind."

"And he imprinted on me… while I was an infant. Which means what exactly?"

"As Nelda mentioned in the vision," Aisha said patiently. "He infected you with his nature. As you know, Elders are the original vampires. Vampires as most humans think of them—like yourself—are simply mutations of these Elders. Humans who have been infected with their dark nature. Usually, the infection causes them to turn into a bloodsucker. But due to the uniqueness of your DNA, that Elder was able to insert some of himself inside of you without you actually turning. So you appeared to be just like a normal human. As you can understand, this was incredibly valuable—the Elders were able to inhabit you, and use your eyes and ears to understand the workings of Arron's mind. You were effectively their ally, even as a baby… Of course, then your parents managed to steal you away from Aviary, and so the

Elders' plan to use you as one of their soldiers never came to fruition."

"Because I was gone before the war actually started," I muttered.

"Yes."

"And my symptoms are so extreme because I was directly touched by an Elder?"

Aisha nodded. "And as a child, at that. The Elder's nature has been ingrained in your system since you were a newborn—from just days after your birth. His nature has become so deep-seated in your veins that when you finally did turn into a vampire and were able to manifest all the symptoms, they have appeared more violently than anyone else you know."

My head was spinning. I had been infected with this sickness directly by one of the most powerful Elders of all time. It was no wonder I was experiencing such problems. Even my father hadn't been infected directly by one of those shadowy creatures. It had been Gregor, his own father, who had turned him.

I recalled the last words the Elder had spoken in

the first vision I'd had back in The Shade.

"Take him back to Aviary... His time will come."

"His time will come," I said out loud. "But my time never came. Because my parents rescued me from Aviary before I could be of use."

"Precisely," Aisha said with a small smile.

"And then the oracle's prediction also came true... When my mother was in the supernatural realm recently, she found out the result of the war that erupted between the Elders and the Hawks. She was told that the two sides attacked each other so viciously that they both finished each other off... And now neither of them are a force to be reckoned with."

"That is what happened," Aisha said.

"But if I had stayed in Aviary longer," I continued, "then it's likely that the Elders would have won?"

"According to the oracle... She saw that you could have been a great tool in discovering the inner workings of Aviary's battalion."

"Do you have any more visions to show me?" I asked, sitting back down on the edge of my armchair.

Aisha shook her head.

So that's it…

I still felt partly in shock. It felt like I had been searching for answers for the longest time, and now I'd discovered the mystery of my past all at once, in a series of visions that had come in quick succession. Supposedly they had the answers as to how I could cure myself, but I still had no clue as to how to go about that.

"But how do I actually solve this?" I said, my insides in knots. "How do I disinfect myself? I'm too far gone. Even the cure didn't work."

To my horror, Aisha simply shrugged. "I'm not sure about that, Benjamin. I was able to reveal things about your past, but I don't know how to actually solve your problem… Honestly? I don't even know if it's possible."

Her words carved a hole in my stomach.

No. There has to be a way out of this. Even if I'm stuck with these jinn, I'm not going to live for the rest of my existence as this crazy bloodsucker.

There just has to be a way.

"What about your aunt?" I asked, even though Nuriya had already told me she didn't know how to cure me.

"You already discussed this matter with her, Ben… She doesn't know how to solve your problem. We can give you information and knowledge, but we can't always guarantee solutions."

What use are information and knowledge without a solution?

"That oracle," I said suddenly. "Hortencia. She's supposed to be all-knowing and all-seeing? Surely she would have some insight as to how to cure me. Is she still living?"

"Yes," Aisha said, bringing some semblance of relief to my churning insides. "She is. Hortencia is actually the love child of a jinni and a witch. Jinn and witches have a long history of hostility toward one another. They usually avoid each other at all costs, and the two species are never supposed to mate. However, Hortencia's parents… somehow or other, they fell in love and out came the creature that became known as 'the oracle'… Actually, two creatures. They gave birth to twins. Pythia and Hortencia. I have never seen Pythia and don't know much about her state, but Hortencia... She is deformed in many ways—for example, she has no eyes. But although physically blind, she has been gifted with sight like no other. By now she is older than anyone knows, but she is still living."

Jinn and witches being natural enemies—this explained why they had turned our witches into birds at the first opportunity, rather than keep and mark them like they had done with vampires, half-bloods and humans. I wondered if, since both species were able to wield magic, the jinn felt threatened by witches—and perhaps vice versa. Now that I thought of it, maybe this was also the reason why Jeramiah's atrium held so few witches.

Of course, more than any of this, I was filled with relief to hear that Hortencia was still alive.

"Do you know where to find Hortencia?" I asked.

"She has moved since the Hawks made visits to her... but yes, I know where to find her."

"Then my next wish is that you take me to see

her," I said, standing up again.

"Very well, Benjamin," Aisha said, with almost a touch of weariness in her voice. "Let's hope she will have the answer you seek."

Chapter 21: River

As I stared at the dove, I couldn't believe that she had been Corrine all along. I shuddered to think what might've happened had I not decided to open her cage and try to free her. She might've been stuck in here forever.

Now that I knew who she was, it felt odd to pick her up. I felt the need to ask permission first.

I was also bursting with questions for her, and it was frustrating to not be able to ask any of them. Most of the ink had dried by now, so it wasn't like she could just answer everything by spelling out letters on the floor.

I bent down so that I was closer to her level as she stood on the floor.

"Ben's going to come back soon," I said. "And he will demand that Nuriya, or her niece, turn you back into yourself." I couldn't begin to imagine how traumatized she must be feeling.

There wasn't an awful lot else that I could say while she was still a dove. I looked up at the clock. *Come on, Ben.*

"Shall we, um… clean that ink off you?" I asked, eyeing her ink-stained feet.

I held out my palm, and she stepped onto it. I took her to the bathroom, filled the sink with warm water, and dipped her feet inside, washing them thoroughly. I wasn't sure whether or not the ink would transfer to her witch feet when she turned back, but it was something to do to make me feel less awkward around Corrine as a bird, and pass the time a bit until Ben returned.

I felt confused as to why she was still a bird when

Ben had demanded that all the witches be turned back and allowed to leave The Oasis. *Could the jinn have disobeyed Ben's request?*

I almost jumped for joy when the front door clicked open. *Ben!* He'd only been gone a little over an hour, but I had been with him practically nonstop for the past few months. I had missed him a lot in just this short period of time away from him.

I hurried out of the bathroom to see Ben standing in the doorway. Surprise took over his face as I rushed up to him with the bird.

"This is Corrine!" I exclaimed.

His eyes moved from me, to the dove, then to all the ink on the floor spelling out the witch's name.

His lips parted, and he looked utterly confused. As he moved further into the room, Aisha appeared next to him.

He turned on the jinni. "This is Corrine, one of The Shade's witches?" he asked in disbelief.

"I believe so," Aisha said nonchalantly.

"How… Why…"

"She ventured near The Oasis, and—as we do with

all witches who aren't specifically authorized to come near our home—we turned her into a bird."

Ben fumed. "But I asked that all The Shade's witches be turned back into their original forms and be set free!"

Aisha raised a brow. "Correct me if I'm wrong, but I believe that your exact wording was for all the witches we had captured *in the last hour* to be set free. This witch had arrived near our boundary before then."

I stared at the jinni. *What tricky, devious creatures these are…*

Ben still looked highly irritated. "I see I have to be careful not to give you people any loopholes in the future," he said. He fixed his eyes back on the dove. "Well, whatever the case, turn Corrine back into herself."

Aisha looked reluctantly at the dove, then heaved a sigh.

"Okay," she said in the most unenthusiastic voice possible.

A moment later, the dove had vanished, and

Corrine—her thick brown hair disheveled, and her face filled with sheer relief—stood before us.

She looked gratefully at me and Ben, and then glared at the jinni.

"So you came here…" Ben said, staring at Corrine.

"Yes," Corrine said breathlessly. "I'd guessed jinn were behind the marks on your arms. The symptoms, along with all the strange happenings that you and River had described, led me to believe that you'd been claimed by jinn, but I didn't want to say anything until I was completely sure. I was holding out hope that just perhaps, it was some kind of powerful witch playing tricks on you… So I came to the desert, but before I could carry out my test, I was caught by one of *these*." She looked pointedly at Aisha, as though Aisha was a speck of dirt on her shoe.

Aisha returned the glare.

"Ibrahim was searching everywhere for you in The Shade," Ben said. "He was pushing for us to stay until you returned, but we just couldn't wait any longer."

"Well, turns out it's a good thing you ended up coming. God knows what would have happened to me if River hadn't discovered me." Her face tensed. "Where is Ibrahim? And why exactly did you come back here?"

Ben filled Corrine in on all that had happened since we left the island, and our decisions behind coming here. The witch looked utterly horrified when Ben revealed the bond he had forged with the jinn. She asked him countless questions and uttered several curses, until finally, Ben arrived at what I was most anxious to hear about—a recounting of the visions he had just witnessed with Aisha.

Both Corrine and I had the same expressions on our faces when Ben was done explaining. Astonishment. Disbelief. Fear.

"I can't believe it," Corrine said. "How do we know all this is for real and it's not just a fabrication of these jinn's imagination?"

"Well, it makes sense, doesn't it?" Ben said. "It explains why I am different from everyone else, and the problems that I've been having. I don't see what reason the jinn have to lie to me about any of this. Besides, this was one of my wishes. Just as I am bound to the jinn, they are obliged to fulfill my desires to the best of their capacity. And I didn't ask for a pack of lies. I asked for the truth about my past." He glanced at Aisha, then looked back at the witch. "I really don't think this is a lie."

"Damn Kiev…" Corrine muttered. "What are you planning to do now?" Her question disappointed me. I'd been hoping that she would make some suggestion to Ben. I looked up at him.

"I've requested Aisha to take me to see Hortencia," he replied. "It's the only thing I can think to do right now. As she's an oracle, if she can't help me, I honestly don't know who can."

"Where does this oracle live?" I asked.

All eyes shot toward Aisha.

"In a secret dwelling that none of you would ever find without me transporting you there," the jinni replied tersely.

Ben addressed the witch. "Have you ever heard of this Hortencia before?"

Corrine looked at him blankly and shrugged. "No. I've never heard of her."

Aisha rolled her eyes. "Well, it's not like she goes out much. There aren't many people who do know of her existence."

"So what do you want to do now, Corrine?" Ben asked. "I think you should return to The Shade. I can have these jinn free you."

To my surprise, Corrine hesitated.

"Ibrahim must be sick with worry by now," Ben pressed.

Corrine bit her lip, looking conflicted. "I know how much Ibrahim will be worrying," she said. "But... No." The doubt that had been in her eyes just a few moments before was replaced with resoluteness. "I will stay with the two of you. I think you need all the help you can get."

Ben shifted on his feet, looking frustrated. "I have these jinn to help me. I don't need you. I want you to return. And I wish River would go back with you." His eyes fell on me, revealing a sense of urgency. "We've reached a fork in the road. I don't know where this path will lead me now, River. Please, just return."

I'd already made it amply clear that I was staying with him, so I wished that he wouldn't bring up the subject again. It seemed that Corrine was just as determined as me.

"No, Ben. I'll stay with you," she said. "I-I still feel partly responsible for what's happened to you. If only I had been more alert that night and vanished before Kiev could snatch you from my arms…"

Ben looked at the witch in exasperation. "Beating yourself up over that is just moronic, Corrine. Stop it."

"All the same," she said, her determination unwavering, "I'll stay."

Then Ben looked down at me in one final attempt to plead with me to return. I just looked up at him like he was stupid for even thinking that I might have changed my mind.

He heaved a sigh. "All right… Aisha, let's go pay a visit to Hortencia."

Chapter 22: Ben

We arrived on the ledge of a cliff overlooking a beach scattered with boulders. It was daytime, but the weather was overcast. The wind was blustery and so bitingly cold even I noticed. I stared out at the sea—or perhaps it was an ocean—wondering where on earth we had just arrived... Then again, maybe we had left Earth.

"Where are we exactly?" River asked, even as she wrapped her arms around herself and shivered. "Are we still in the human realm?"

I wished there was something I could do to warm her up. I wanted to hold her close, but that would only make her colder. I was grateful when Corrine removed the shawl from her shoulders and wrapped it around River.

"If you must know"—Aisha scowled—"yes, we are still on Earth. We are on the west coast of Canada."

"Canada," River muttered, gazing around the shore.

Thankfully, there wasn't a human in sight.

Aisha turned her back on the ocean, and moved toward the face of the cliff. I realized as she approached a narrow crack in the wall that Hortencia obviously had a certain taste in the dwellings she chose. I squeezed through the crack, River and Corrine following after me. We found ourselves moving through a damp, narrow tunnel—not unlike the one I had seen in the vision. It wound this way and that until we reached the end where, no surprise, there was a moldy-looking door. The four of us stopped and gathered round it.

"When was the last time you saw this woman?" I

asked Aisha.

"I have never met her before, but my aunt has," the jinni replied. "I'm not sure when Nuriya last saw her… But in case you're worried about whether she still lives here, don't worry. She's here. Hortencia?" Aisha raised her voice. "It is Aisha Nasiri. I mean you no harm. I have come with friends. We would like to ask you a few questions, if you would be so kind as to let us in."

My ears picked up on a faint grumbling on the other side of the door. Then there was the clinking of keys and the heavy door clicked open. As the door creaked open, the shadowy form of the oracle appeared before us.

She looked identical to the person I'd seen in the vision. Despite her apparent youth, she had the same almost-bald head, symbol-inked skin, strange silver visor covering her eyes, and unless I remembered wrong, she was even wearing the same dark green colored robe.

She froze in the doorway, her lips pursing. River looked part intrigued, part terrified by the woman. I held my breath as, slowly, she raised a small hand and hovered it upward, directly toward Corrine, who was standing outside the oracle's front door.

"Who have we here?" Hortencia spoke in a low voice. "A frazzled witch." She moved her outstretched hand so that it pointed next at Aisha. "A jealous jinni." Aisha stiffened. Hortencia pointed at River. "An infatuated half-blood." A flush of red rose in River's cheeks as she avoided my gaze.

Finally, the tips of Hortencia's fingers grazed my chest. But as they did, she withdrew her hand abruptly as though she'd gotten an electric shock. She turned her body to face me directly, her head tilting upward. "And, oh, my... A vampire seeking answers. We have met before, boy... Benjamin Novak. The imprinted."

The imprinted. I was relieved that at least she brought us straight to the subject.

"Hortencia," I said, "I'm glad to meet you." I considered holding out my hand to shake, but given the reaction she'd had to touching me, I thought it wise to keep my hands by my side.

She backed through the doorway, gesturing with a flick of her hand that we follow her.

We stepped into a small cave that was so austere it didn't look fit for habitation by anyone but an animal. There was an old thin mattress laid out on the floor in one corner, covered with some grubby sheets and patchwork blankets. Lining one of the walls were makeshift shelves containing an array of strange objects—some of which appeared to be crystal orbs. There was a narrow table with a missing leg, at which a wooden chair was pulled up. Then there was an area which could hardly be called a kitchen, although clearly she prepared food there. There was an ancient-looking stove and on the floor was a small pile of unwashed pots, plates and spoons.

There was nowhere for us to sit, since she sat down on the only chair available, and so we remained standing—or in Aisha's case, hovering.

An awkward silence fell between us as the oracle, behind her silver visor, continued to face my direction.

I cleared my throat. "You know who I am," I said.

"And I need help from you. How does one disinfect oneself from the nature of the Elders after being imprinted upon? Is it even—"

Before I could finish my sentence, she began shaking her head forcefully. Then she shot to her feet. "No, no, no!" Her voice was bizarrely loud, even as she continued to shake her head so hard, I wondered if she hadn't made herself dizzy by now. "You're asking the wrong question, boy!"

The look of genuine fury in her face took me aback.

The wrong question? What?

As brilliant as this woman might be, she was clearly stark raving mad.

I had no idea what to make of her response. That was the only question I needed an answer to. *What does she mean, wrong question?* I was scared for a moment that perhaps this was her reaction to not knowing the answer. That perhaps she couldn't help me either.

But then she spoke again. Her voice was calmer this time, and she sat back down in the chair sideways, her arm resting over the back of it.

"Rephrase your question," she said.

I looked toward my three companions, wondering if they had any clue what she meant. Even Aisha looked clueless.

"I'm sorry," I said. "I'm not sure what you mean. I just need to find out how to solve my problem."

"Why don't you ask me why you're infected to begin with? You might find that leads you in the right direction…" she said, clasping her hands together on her lap.

"But I've already been shown why—"

Hortencia let out a wild giggle. "Oh, you've only seen the dribs and drabs that this little jinni managed to show you… Just ask me the question, vampire."

"Okay," I said, even as I felt thoroughly disconcerted. "Why was I infected to begin with?"

A contented smile spread across her lips.

"Because those creatures of shadow wanted you as part of their army."

To my confusion, she paused.

Is that all she's got for me?

"Uh, I already know that—"

"No, you don't," she snapped, her mild expression turning sharp again. "You don't know."

I breathed in. "Then please tell me what I don't know."

"Their use for you as an infant was only half of their plan."

I froze.

"What?"

She reached behind her, toward one of the makeshift shelves, and pulled off what appeared to be a crystal ball, small enough to fit within the palm of her hand.

She rolled it between her palms and began dropping it from one to the other absentmindedly. I wasn't sure if the ball was at all required for what she was explaining to me. It looked like she was just playing with it, taking her time and enjoying keeping us all on edge.

"What?" I repeated, unable to hide the urgency in my voice.

She coughed, then, to my relief, continued. "The

Elders took to heart my suspicion that neither they nor the Hawks would survive the battle that sparked between them. And so when you came along… they saw much potential. That Elder did more than just insert his nature within you so that you could be useful to them during the battle. In case you managed to survive while his—and his companions'—strength faded, he intended for you to grow up and retain his essence long into the future."

"What do you mean by essence?" I asked, barely louder than a whisper.

Ignoring my question, she stood up suddenly. The ball dropped to the floor and shattered, sending shards flying everywhere. Her face contorted, growing tight with a kind of manic intensity. "Your time is coming, Benjamin Novak. Soon."

"Your time is coming."

The moment she said the words, the whispery voice of the Elder rang through my head as I recalled the words he'd spoken in the first vision.

"What do you mean, his time is coming?" River asked, terrified, as she clasped my hand.

Without warning, the oracle lurched forward and grabbed River's arm. I was about to knock the woman aside, but after a few seconds it became clear that she meant no harm. The strange black symbols on her skin began to migrate and shift their shape as she said in a strained whisper, "I mean, girl, that very soon this man may not be the same one you fell for."

"Enough of this nonsense!" Corrine exploded. Raising a palm, she shot the oracle backward across the room. Hortencia crumpled in a heap on the mattress.

I stared at Corrine in shock. "What are you doing?" I gasped, grabbing the witch's hand and forcing it down to her side, even though it was too late.

Corrine ignored me, still fuming at the oracle. "For Christ's sake, can't you just talk normally? Explain slowly and calmly what on earth you're talking about. You're scaring the hell out of these kids!"

I suspected from Corrine's outburst that it wasn't just us *kids* the oracle was "scaring the hell out of".

The oracle looked shaken by the fall, even though

she had landed on her bed. She huddled up in a corner, drawing her short legs up against her chest and shutting her lips tight.

I glared at Corrine.

"You shouldn't have done that, witch," Aisha said. "She might close up now and refuse to reveal any more information."

Corrine scowled.

As a hushed silence fell about the chamber, I feared perhaps Aisha's words might come true.

I swallowed hard, then looked toward Corrine, Aisha and River.

"I think it's best if the three of you step outside and leave the two of us alone to talk."

Although I had phrased it as a suggestion, I didn't give any of them the chance to protest. I ushered them out of the room and then closed the door behind them. They would stand just outside, and it wasn't like they wouldn't be able to hear everything that we said anyway.

Then I turned around again, my eyes falling on the oracle who was still closed up in a corner like a clam.

I approached her cautiously. I stopped about three feet away from her and lowered myself to her level.

"Please," I said, in as calm a voice as I could manage. "I need you to explain to me exactly what you're saying."

I feared that she was about to go on another manic tirade, but I was relieved when this time her voice was much steadier as she spoke, although her words were no less chilling.

"You will understand soon what I'm talking about. The symptoms will begin to manifest."

"Hortencia, I'm already experiencing the symptoms that…"

My voice trailed off as the oracle shook her head slowly, a look of melancholy taking over her face.

"Oh, no, vampire. The symptoms you've experienced so far have been simply the tip of the iceberg."

CHAPTER 23: BEN

Simply the tip of the iceberg.

It felt like my world was crashing down around me. Feeling unsteady, I grabbed hold of the rocky wall for support. My throat felt so dry it was painful to swallow.

Hortencia stretched out her legs and stood up. She moved back to her chair and sat down at the table, her palms spread out flat against the surface, her back turned toward me.

"What most who venture here don't realize is that

seeing is a curse, not a gift," she said softly. "Something to be repulsed by, not desired... Do you really want to know exactly what's up ahead of you, boy? Glimpsing the future is not conducive to the health or happiness one still has a chance to grasp in the present."

"I need to know," I rasped. I walked over to the table so that I could see her face, and planted my own hands down in front of hers. "Please, tell me."

She inhaled deeply. Then, to my surprise, she removed the silver visor from her eyes for the first time... only to reveal that she possessed no eyes. Where they should have been was just smooth, pale flesh. I tried not to let on to my horror, but I was sure that she sensed it. A small smile appeared on her lips.

"I would any day swap my unbounded knowledge of the universe for mortal eyes... But I see your mind is bent on your request."

She stood up from the chair and then grabbed my arm, her grasp surprisingly strong. She pulled me down to sit in her seat while she remained standing at the opposite end of the table.

Goosebumps ran along my skin as she began, "Let me start by telling you something of the war that broke out between the Elders and the Hawks. You heard that the two sides fought each other so severely that both were left with a crumbling kingdom. But you don't know exactly how the Elders were weakened, and understanding this is key to understanding your own situation." She walked over to the stove and planted a pot on top of it. Grabbing a jug, she poured in some murky-looking water and lit a fire beneath it.

I wished that she would just sit down and give me her full attention.

"When it came time for the two sides to go at each other's throats, so to speak," she continued, "while the Hawks were planning their attack on Cruor, they knew that they had to take a twofold approach: destroy the vessels the Elders had remaining, as well as ruin their vast supply of blood. Remember at this time, the Elders and Hawks believed that all the gates leading to Earth had been closed. Given that, the

Hawks believed that if they managed to wipe out the majority of the Elders' vessels—who they used in combat—as well as their blood, the Elders' strength would evaporate."

She paused, raising a thin brow, as if prompting me to ask any questions on what she had said so far.

"How did they get so much human blood to begin with?" I asked.

"During all those years those spirits had access to Earth, they amassed an enormous supply of blood and stored it within the bowels of their black mountains."

"Elders don't have a physical body," I said, trying to remember what my parents had told me of the subject. "What use to them is blood? I don't understand why they would have so much."

"For Elders, blood epitomizes energy and life. It's their food, their sustenance, and without it, they are reduced to more or less dormant spirits. Elders draw life from blood in two ways—the first being via a vessel. That is, a human they have turned into a vampire—a mutation of themselves. They are able to enter the infected human and use his senses to relish the blood as if they were the Elder's own. Secondly, even without vessels, Elders can draw benefit from it. Since blood is the very essence of what life is for them, just being within close proximity of the substance, even though not able to consume it directly, gives them strength. Consequently, the Hawks targeted these two things—vessels, whom they used not only in combat but also to consume blood, and then the masses of blood itself."

"And they were successful?" I asked.

"It was a slow, painful battle," Hortencia replied, pouring out the hot water into a metal cup and moving back toward the table. She picked up the visor that she had left there and replaced it to cover her eyeless face. "But yes, eventually the Hawks managed to wipe out many—if not most of—the vessels, and then contaminated every single one of their blood chambers."

"How did they contaminate all that blood?"

"With an insidious poison that they obtained from the merfolk. There are a number of venomous species that inhabit the deep waters surrounding The Cove. They invaded the merfolk's home temporarily until they'd farmed enough of the poison."

"So the Hawks destroyed their army of vessels along with all their blood—"

"But all this came at a price, of course," Hortencia interrupted. "In achieving this, the Hawks lost most of their own army. Their greatest leaders and strongest warriors... except Arron himself. Arron survived, although gravely injured. The Elders, although technically still living, are also greatly weakened, and without blood, or any vessels that they could use to procure more, those spirits retreated into their mountains, debilitated, where they still remain today."

I was so engrossed in what Hortencia was telling me, hanging onto her every word, I was forgetting to breathe.

"Now you're wondering what all of this has to do with you," she said. "Well, it has everything to do with you." She paused, blowing against the surface of her hot water, before taking a small sip. Then, picking up the cup in her hands, she began to pace slowly up and down the small room. "Before the war, the Elders knew what the Hawks intended to do in order to vanquish them. They knew they were after their vessels and blood. It was for this reason that one of the leaders—Basilius, as some call him—saw the opportunity to infect your soul, imprint on you so that he could inhabit you, and then he did... a little more than that. I should say, a lot more than that... He *bonded* himself with you."

My voice caught in my throat. *"What?"*

"He created a link between your soul and his. A link that could make you feel his presence, no matter how far apart you might be."

My head spun. "Y-You're telling me, all this time, since days after my birth, an Elder has been... present inside me?"

"Indeed. Since the day that Elder touched you as a newborn, the bond he forged has remained deep within you."

"That makes no sense! How could I have not known? How could I have not sensed his presence?"

The oracle smiled a little. "But I think that you have sensed him, haven't you? You see, boy, the Elder himself is not physically inside of you. He has been too weak to actually fully possess you, and besides, he is still in Cruor. But he created a window into your soul. A window through which he is able to touch you... and you have felt his presence. He manifests himself most strongly after you've made a kill. You've felt his presence closing in on you after you've murdered. That's the very reason that you went to The Oasis to begin with—so that you wouldn't have to kill in order to get human blood. Am I not right?"

My mind reeled as her words sank in.

It did make sense. Too much sense for comfort.

"A-And I can only stomach human blood—"

"Because that's what your stomach is meant to consume. Your stomach is meant to be *his* stomach."

My heart skipped a beat.

"And I... I couldn't turn back into a human—"

"That's right," the oracle replied. "Because you are not meant to turn back. The Elder has claimed you as his own, and it's his influence that is keeping you as a vampire."

Horror filled me. "Can he read my thoughts?"

"Occasionally, I'm sure, and that will only increase with time," she replied.

"With time? Why is he even bonded with me to begin with? What good will his presence within me do for him?"

"You are his lifeline, Benjamin. With every mouthful of human blood that you swallow, you are nursing him back to health. The bond he created with you means he can benefit from the blood you consume. His weakened soul is being revived. Strengthened. Your feeding is his feeding…"

I sat, gaping at the woman.

"You've been downing human blood for some months now," she continued. "It won't be much longer now until the scale tips and he becomes strong enough."

"Strong enough for what?" I breathed.

"Strong enough to manipulate your actions even when you're not under the influence of bloodlust… Strong enough to call you back to him in Cruor. I believe you are only days away from it."

"And do what with me exactly?"

"Well, once one of those creatures has gained strength—especially one as influential as Basilius—it becomes easier for the others to recover too. Especially with your help."

I racked my brain to recall the stories my parents had recounted to me of when the Elders had taken over The Shade. If I remembered right, Corrine had managed to exorcise a number of Elders from our people. And Odelia, the Ageless at the time, had freed my mother from the grasp of one of them.

"So now I know about his influence over me," I said, trying to steady my voice, "I just need a witch to help me get rid of it."

My heart sank to the pit of my stomach as the oracle shook her head. "I'm afraid the situation is much more… subtle than that," she replied. "Because the Elder's presence has been with you your whole life—practically since the day you were born—he has become ingrained in your system… almost one with you. He has been with you far too long for any spell to be effective. And I should warn you that any such attempt to exorcise him with magic could have fatal consequences for you—especially because, as I said, his soul currently remains safely in Cruor."

My hands shook. I shot to my feet, causing the chair to clatter against the floor behind me.

"You need to help get this thing away from me," I said, my heart pounding. "Please."

She looked at me calmly, then swallowed back the last of her water.

"I don't know how to do that," she said.

"What do you mean…" My voice trailed off as I paused, staring at her. "What do you see of my future?"

"I see your future clearly," she said. "And I see only one path. The path you were destined for the night the Elder engulfed your soul with his." She planted a hand on my shoulder, sadness taking hold of her soft features, before she spoke her final words to me:

"Whether you like it or not, Benjamin, the time has come for you to take your place. Your place as their soldier of shadows."

CHAPTER 24: RIVER

Listening to every horrifying word this oracle spoke, I couldn't stand to remain outside the room any longer. Grabbing the handle, I forced the door open and rushed inside. Benjamin was standing at the opposite end of the room, looking stunned, his face paler than I'd ever seen it, while Hortencia stood a few feet away, holding a cup in her hands.

"Destiny can be changed," I said, stumbling forward and clutching the woman's shoulders.

It infuriated me when she didn't respond. She just

had a blank expression as she faced me.

I shook her, trying to force a response. "Am I not right? There *must* be some way out of this."

Still, she didn't respond. Her lips pressed together, forming a hard line.

Corrine entered the room after me, followed by Aisha. Corrine looked just as dumbstruck as I felt.

Seeing that the oracle was refusing to give me any relief, I rushed up to Ben and threw my arms around his shoulders. I pressed my head against his chest, shutting my eyes tight.

No. No. This isn't happening. This can't be happening. Not to Ben. My Ben.

Ben's hands traveled down my arms until they slid to my hands and he detached me from him. I looked up at his face, hating how stoic it had become. He swallowed hard. He looked like a man who'd just been given his death sentence.

He remained staring at Hortencia for several moments, then nodded slightly toward her before taking my hand and leading me to the door. I dug my heels against the floor, trying to keep myself rooted to the spot. I didn't want to leave this place until we had an answer from this woman.

Ben turned around. "River, let's go."

"How can we just go?" I said, my voice shaking. "After what you've just learned? We can't just go. Dammit, I don't believe Hortencia doesn't have any answers."

"You heard what she said," he said, his voice deep. "She has already given me her answer."

His gaze traveled to Corrine, who looked speechless, and then fell on Aisha, to whom he nodded briefly.

"Take us back to The Oasis."

"No!"

But it was too late. The cave vanished, and we reappeared in the living room of Benjamin's apartment back in the jinn's atrium. Tears of panic moistened my eyes, my whole body trembling.

"Ben," I gasped. "What are you going to do?"

He paused, his eyes darkening. "I need to abstain from consuming any more blood for as long as I possibly can. And I need to think."

I looked desperately at Aisha and Corrine. "Don't either of you have any idea how to get rid of that thing from Ben?"

Both of them looked at each other blankly before shaking their heads.

"I've never come across anything like this before," Corrine croaked. "An Elder bonding with a human newborn, remaining with him all the way until adulthood, and then through your turning into a vampire... This is utterly unheard of to me."

"As I said," Ben said to me quietly. "I need to think... And I'd like to be alone for some time."

"O-Okay," I said. I motioned to leave the room along with Corrine and Aisha, but Ben caught my arm.

"No, River. I would like you to stay with me, but just... Corrine and Aisha, if you could give me some space."

I was grateful that he'd held me back while the others left the room. I didn't know that I could stand to be apart from him at a time like this.

After Corrine and Aisha left the apartment, Ben

held my trembling hand in his. His hand was also shaking slightly, although I could see he was trying to hold steady. He walked with me to his bedroom. He sat on the edge of his bed. I inched closer to him. Standing between his legs and positioning his hands around me, I moved in to hug him. I held his head in my arms, resting it against my chest as I dropped silent tears into his hair. Breathing in his scent, I kissed the top of his head.

We remained silent—I wasn't sure what either of us could say. We'd arrived at a dead end as far as I could see. From what Ben had revealed, it appeared that the only plan he had was to try to delay the Elder's influence as long as possible. Avoid drinking more blood. But I knew how difficult that was for him. He wouldn't be able to go without it for long before his bloodlust took hold of him and he went storming through the prison cells above until he'd quenched his thirst.

I lost track of how long I stood there, holding him in my arms as he held me. I was trying to draw some kind of strength from him, but it felt as though he

A SOLDIER OF SHADOWS

was slipping through my fingers.

Finally I broke the silence.

"How exactly do you think your symptoms will worsen? She said that you'd become... practically unrecognizable."

I felt his chest heave against me as he let out a deep sigh. Then he placed his hands on my hips and created a distance between us. His face was ashen, but otherwise unnervingly unreadable.

"It's late," was all he responded with. "We both should get some rest."

Rest? I didn't understand how he could think about rest. At that moment I'd rather do anything in the world other than sleep.

But I didn't argue with him. Instead I just nodded, gulping.

Perhaps the events of the day really had taken a toll on Ben's stamina. After those visions Aisha had given him, and then the trauma he'd just been through in the cave of the oracle, I guessed that I shouldn't have been surprised if he was exhausted. I thought that perhaps he might want to sleep without me, have some time on his own to collect his thoughts, but before I could suggest that I sleep in one of the spare bedrooms, he gathered me to him and stood up. He carried me around the bed and laid me gently down against the pillows. Then he lowered himself next to me and enveloped me in his arms. I twined my legs with his and raised a hand to his cheek, my fingers brushing against the roughness of his jawline.

My face level with his, I stared deep into his green eyes. He moved his head closer to me on the pillow and pressed his lips against mine in a slow, tender kiss. I shut my eyes, wanting to lose myself in that kiss. Wanting this moment to be ingrained in my memory forever. And wanting to wake up tomorrow by his side only for this to all have been a horrible dream.

His thumb brushed against my cheek as he wiped away a tear that had slipped from the corner of my eye.

His voice was hoarse as he spoke. "I can't tell you that I know what I'm going to do. I don't. I haven't the slightest clue where we go from here, or even if there is anywhere to go but in the same direction I've been veering toward ever since I tasted my first drop of human blood." His voice lowered. "But River..." His lips moved closer until they grazed mine as he whispered, "I need to tell you that I'm in love with you."

My breath hitched. His words were a shot of ecstasy straight to my heart. The joy that erupted in my chest spread through my entire body, making my skin tingle, my blood pound. I felt like I was soaring above the waves of fear I'd been drowning in since our visit to the oracle and up toward a never-ending sky.

I gazed into Ben's intense green eyes as they bored into mine. And I revealed the depths of my own heart for the first time.

"I love you, Ben," I whispered.

Chapter 25: Ben

Hearing the same words from her own lips was something I hadn't been prepared for. Although they filled me with a level of euphoria I'd never experienced before, I wished she hadn't said it back. A part of me even wished that she didn't feel the same way. That she could have just absorbed my words and nodded politely.

Because now that she'd bared her feelings to me, it would make what I had to do all the harder.

I shouldn't have told her, but I couldn't stop

myself. I didn't know when, or if, I would see her again after that night. And after everything we'd been through, and after falling for her so hard, I just couldn't bring myself to leave without telling her the truth. Even if it would only cause the two of us more pain.

As she held my face, pushing her lips against mine, I wanted nothing more than to just lose myself in her. Even if only for the next hour.

But even in this, I knew that I could only go so far.

Sliding my hands through her silky brown hair, I gazed into the depths of her beautiful turquoise eyes. Tears moistened the sides of them, but deep within them burnt desire. Need. Her hands left the sides of my face and she began unbuttoning my shirt. I was too consumed by her kiss to bring myself to stop her. She loosened the shirt and tugged it off my shoulders. As our lips broke apart for a few seconds, she whispered, "Don't leave me, Ben. I need you."

My throat felt dry. Although I'd been trying to

hide my intention, it seemed she knew me too well to not have picked up on my mood.

Leave River.

Hearing those words spoken out loud made it seem real. Cemented. No longer just a plan in my head, but something inevitable, almost something that had already happened. Although I knew I had no choice, I wasn't ready to hear it yet.

I felt an ache deep inside as I saw the pain behind her eyes.

Dipping down, I kissed her intensely, with more heat than ever before. She planted her palms against my shoulders and pushed until we were both kneeling upright on the bed. Catching my hands, she placed them behind her neck, over the top of her dress zipper. As I brushed my lips beneath her ear, I gripped the zipper and glided it down her back until she was free from the dress.

I knew that I needed to stop somewhere about here, but River was like a drug to me. Her smooth skin. Her captivating gaze. Her soft, intense breathing... I couldn't tear my eyes away from her as she lay down against the pillows, looking up at me through her long dark lashes with her hair splayed out beneath her.

I lifted her up and turned her around so that her back pressed against my chest, the graceful shape of her melding against the front of me.

Sweeping aside her hair, I rested a hand over her bare navel, while my other arm wrapped around her midriff. I pressed slow kisses against the back of her neck, trailing them down the backs of her shoulders. I felt her shiver as my lips passed over the bump of her bra and grazed the length of her spine.

I pushed her back against the pillows. Crouching down over her, I closed my mouth around hers and brushed my tongue against the tip of hers. The soft moan she let out, followed by her hands pulling me closer, electrified me. Kneeling on the bed in the space between her thighs, I relished exploring her body, kissing around the outline of her bra, making my way down her abdomen, and stopping just above the line of her panties.

The desire I felt for her was burning within me. I wanted nothing more than to spend all night exploring every part of her.

But as she reached behind her to unclasp her bra, I caught them and held them in place.

I couldn't allow her to give me this. Not when I had no idea whether I'd even see her after tonight.

I loved her too much to take this from her.

She gazed up at me, her lips and cheeks flushed with passion. A look of confusion played across her face, her dark brows frowning slightly.

I couldn't offer her an explanation. Instead, running my hands from her ribcage down the curve of her waist, I caressed the softness of her chest with my lips before raising my head and meeting her eyes.

It killed me to think that she might be doubting herself, that she could be thinking that I didn't want her, or that I was rejecting her for some fault of her own.

As much as every fiber of my being raged against the decision, I lay back down against the pillows next to her and spooned myself around her.

I felt her disappointment as she sighed against me.

I planted a soft kiss against the back of her head and began brushing a palm over her forehead, hoping that it would aid sleep. Her muscles relaxed against me as I continued stroking her.

It was a couple of hours before sleep finally took her, and just before it did, as she was half in, half out of consciousness, she whispered those words again.

"I love you."

Chapter 26: Ben

As River's steady breathing became deeper, I slipped out of bed. I picked up the shirt she'd removed from me and put it on. Then I moved noiselessly to the door that I had left slightly ajar to avoid creaking. Before heading out of the room completely, I allowed my eyes to linger on her beautiful, almost-bare form one last time.

She was curled up in a fetal position, the same position she'd been in while my body had been enveloping her. As if she never wanted to let go of me.

She would've come with me in a heartbeat wherever this path would lead me, and that was precisely why I couldn't warn her I was leaving. I had allowed her to stay with me once, but this time... this time I just couldn't.

For all I knew, in a matter of days I might not even recognize her anymore. Heck, I might not even recognize myself. I didn't know exactly how it would happen. But even though I would try to avoid drinking more blood, I wasn't stupid enough to think that I could do that for long. I doubted I'd be able to keep it up for more than a few days—at the very most. That was when my bloodlust usually took hold of me and turned me into a wild animal, willing to do anything and murder anyone until I got my fill.

Although River was a half-blood, for all I knew, once the oracle's prediction came true I might become a danger even to her.

Leaving the bedroom, I swept along the corridor, trying to figure out which of the spare rooms Corrine had retreated into. I caught the witch's scent and stopped outside one that had an orange glow emanating from the crack beneath its door.

My knuckles made contact with the wood in the softest knock. I heard footsteps, and a moment later, Corrine had eased the door open and stood before me in a nightgown.

Clearly, she hadn't been able to sleep. I stepped into the room with her, pushing the door softly behind me.

I cleared my throat, bracing myself for her reaction. "Corrine. I need you to go back to The Shade with River. I need you to leave and not come back."

Her mouth fell open, a mixture of anxiety and confusion in her eyes. "But Ben, River and I already told you that we're staying with you through this."

As a much as I appreciated Corrine's loyalty, I wished that she would just agree and not fight me on this. After the evening with River, I felt emotionally drained.

"Things are different now," I said. "I've already made up my mind." I reached out and touched

Corrine's shoulder. "Please," I said. "Just return with River."

She bit down hard on her lower lip. Then she stepped away from me, clasping a palm to her forehead. "I'm so terrified for you, Benjamin," she said, sinking down on the bed. "I just wish that there was some way I could use my magic to help you in all this."

"Corrine." Crouching down until my face was level with hers, I reached for her hands. I held them, giving them a small squeeze. "You couldn't do more for me than you already have. Thank you for staying with me this far."

She looked teary as she nodded, then drew me in for a hug, planting a kiss against the top of my head.

She stood up, drawing in a deep breath.

"Okay," she said, her voice uneven. "I'll take River back now. Do we have permission to leave this place?"

I nodded. "Yes," I said. "I already made sure of that. Listen, River is sleeping in my bed. She's in her underwear, so if you could take her dress with you so she can change once you arrive…"

"Of course." Corrine moved toward the exit of the room, still eyeing me with uncertainty. Then just as she was about to grip the handle, she breathed out sharply and hurried back toward me, pulling me in for another hug. "Oh, Ben, what do you plan to do?"

I heaved a sigh as I stared blankly at the opposite wall over her shoulder.

"I don't know, Corrine," I murmured. "All I know is, this is a journey I have to make alone."

Chapter 27: Derek

To everyone's angst—especially Ibrahim's—Corrine still hadn't returned. Ibrahim became convinced that she must have ventured out to The Oasis, and that she was now stuck there along with Ben. I returned with him to the desert to try to get Ben's attention— although my son believed himself to be trapped there, at least he could have the jinn free Corrine. But nobody came. We could only assume that Ben couldn't hear us and we had no choice but to return to The Shade.

Our belief about what had happened to Corrine only fueled my determination to crack The Oasis.

I couldn't stop thinking about the bond my son had formed with the jinn. I just couldn't accept that there was no way out for him. Perhaps it was all the obstacles and seemingly undefeatable supernaturals that we'd had to deal with in the past, or perhaps it was just my stubbornness, but I was incapable of accepting the situation.

I had no idea where to start, but our island was filled with supernatural creatures from all places and backgrounds. I found it hard to believe that not a single one of them would be able to shed any light on these jinn. So I called for anyone in The Shade who had even the slightest bit of knowledge to step forward and visit me in our penthouse.

It turned out that all of our witches, including Mona, were clueless—never having encountered a jinni in their lives—and so were our vampires, werewolves, and of course our humans, many of whom had spent their whole lives in The Shade and couldn't be expected to know anything else outside of it.

I even tried asking the ogres, who—perhaps predictably—just shrugged and looked at me like I was talking French.

My answer came from an unexpected source— from one of the dragons, Jeriad himself. I was relieved when in the late hour of the evening, he came knocking at the door of my and Sofia's penthouse. He caught me alone, since Sofia was at Vivienne's place—Vivienne was due to give birth any day now.

I opened the door and laid eyes on the imposing dragon shifter standing on the doorstep.

"Jeriad."

"You seek information about jinn."

At first I was surprised that Jeriad had come to see me only now. Then I realized that none of the dragons had examined Ben or River before we left for The Oasis. If they had seen their marks before we took off, they might have been able to guess that it was jinn we were up against.

"Yes," I said eagerly. "Come in."

He stepped inside, his eyes traveling around the living room, before looking back at me. It occurred to me that this was the first time he had ever stepped inside our treehouse. I offered him a seat on the sofa, but he remained standing.

"Back in The Hearthlands, we had some experience with jinn. There was a time when we even made allies out of some."

"What can you tell me about them?"

"For one thing, they are not easy to bargain with," he said. "The jinn inhabiting The Oasis—we have no experience with that particular tribe. But we have had ties with others. We also know where their realm is and how to reach it."

I felt a blow of disappointment. "But not knowing anything about this particular tribe... how could this help my son? He is bound to the jinn of The Oasis, and not to the species as a whole, as he explained it."

The dragon paused, and wet his lower lip thoughtfully.

"That is true," he replied. "But jinn as a species...

they are usually quite interconnected. Many have ties with each other, whether they like it or not."

"What do you mean by ties?"

"It's rather complicated," he said, "and there's not much point me going into detail now when I don't know for sure that what I have in mind would work… but what I'm suggesting is that we pay a visit to their realm with you. Due to the relations we dragons have had with them in the past—at least, our tribe of dragons—the jinn hold some respect for us. There's a certain family of jinn who live there whom I would like to meet with."

I didn't understand exactly how meeting jinn who lived in a different realm could help my son who was trapped on earth in The Oasis. But I trusted Jeriad, and we had nothing else on the table, so I wasn't going to start questioning him.

"So you would take us there?"

Jeriad nodded. "Of course," he continued, "we cannot guarantee your safety. Jinn are subtle, tricky creatures, and even our might is not much good against them. It has been a long time since we've had contact with those creatures, and I'm not sure that they would still welcome us into their midst as they once did. So you must be aware that there is an element of danger involved in the excursion."

I nodded, clenching my jaw.

"Also," he added, after another moment's pause, "I suggest that every single dragon here in The Shade go along."

"Why's that?" I said, feeling uneasy at the idea of such a huge chunk of the island's security taking off at once.

"As I said, I don't know exactly what the jinn's reaction will be to our visit. The minds of jinn are fickle and ever-changing. They can quickly develop dislikes toward others, often for no good reason. It's hard to predict what their temperament might be toward dragons when we arrive. Hence, I suggest we travel in force... and also that no witches travel with us."

"No witches?" Although I was happy for them to remain here on the island to protect our people, I also felt uneasy about embarking on this excursion without even a single wielder of magic. Out of all of our missions in the past, I couldn't recall a single one where we hadn't had at least one witch present.

"Jinn and witches are born enemies. If a witch entered the realm of jinn, it's unlikely that they would ever make it out again, even with our help."

"I see." I looked the dragon in the eye. "I appreciate you stepping forward."

"Although I'm unable to make any promises that we can free your son, I feel we owe you our help. I'm grateful for the hospitality you have extended us, and the happiness many of us have found here with the island's maidens."

I nodded, still caught up on the idea of traveling without witches. "This means everyone who comes will have to travel on your backs."

"Of course," he said. "So… you would definitely like to go through with this? I'll need to speak with my companions."

I would have preferred that my wife was present so I could discuss it with her. But although I still felt uneasy about so many things about this plan—what kind of hostility we might find at our destination, leaving our witches behind, and the fact that I desperately wanted to be here for my sister when she gave birth to my new nephew or niece—I felt that I had no choice but to take the dragon up on his offer there and then, while he was feeling generous. I didn't want to risk delaying my answer in case something caused Jeriad to have second thoughts and withdraw.

And so that night I agreed to the fire breather's plan.

CHAPTER 28: JERAMIAH

I stared down at the injured mermaid I'd found washed up along a beach near The Shade's port. Bending down, I placed a finger against the side of her scaly neck, checking for a pulse. She had one, albeit weak. It was surprising considering the amount of blood she had lost. Her left arm had been ripped open, and the sand beneath her was stained with the dark liquid.

Removing my shirt, I wiped her down, then wrapped the fabric tightly around the gash to help stem the blood flow. I picked her up and hauled her over my shoulders, confident that she was too weak to do anything to harm me as I carried her.

She and a merman had gained entrance to The Shade the same way Amaya, my witch companion, and I had. We had been carried through the boundary via the submarine Benjamin had been navigating. I'd known as soon as Nuriya had revealed to me back in The Oasis that my cousin's submarine held merfolk that they could be of great use to me. I had expected to have to catch them, however. It was a pleasant surprise to see one practically delivered to me on a silver platter. I thanked whatever creature had attacked this mermaid as I made my way back toward the temporary residence Amaya and I had created for ourselves.

I was just approaching the Port when I noticed a crowd of people gathered in the clearing in front of the jetty. I stopped in my tracks. I spotted my uncle, Derek Novak—whom I had identified during my first few days on this island when I had scoped the island out along with its residents.

Next to him stood Sofia herself. Wife of Derek Novak, she'd been the one my father had desired so deeply. And now she was my aunt.

Standing next to the redhead was Vivienne. Now a human, and heavily pregnant. She stood beside her husband—my second uncle—Xavier Vaughn.

I also spotted my cousin, Rose Novak—Benjamin's twin. She stood next to a man whom I'd come to learn was her newlywed husband, Caleb Achilles.

And then there was Aiden Claremont. One of the first of my extended family I'd encountered on arrival. I'd been tempted to stake that vampire as he slept the night I realized who he was. But I was glad that I had refrained from temptation. Acting impulsively would have been detrimental to my plans in the long run...

Behind my family were other vampires and werewolves, most of whom I didn't recognize—and frankly had little interest in—and what appeared to be a crowd of perhaps one hundred dragons. I'd gathered that they had taken up residence in lavish apartments especially carved out for them within the

Black Heights by the witches. I wouldn't have been surprised if every single dragon who inhabited this island had gathered there in the clearing.

They looked fiercely imposing even in their humanoid forms… I'd known from the start that these shifters were my biggest obstacle.

But as I began to pay attention to the conversation my family was having, I was delighted by what I heard.

Derek was addressing Xavier. "We're going to try to make this as brief as possible." His eyes fell on his sister. I'd have to be blind to not notice the adoration he held for his twin. He drew her in for an embrace and kissed her cheek. "Just hang in there, Viv. Xavier will be here, and so will the rest of the witches."

Vivienne cast her eyes nervously toward the dragons. "Must you really take all of them?" she asked.

"It's what Jeriad wants, and since he's leading us there, we can't really argue."

Xavier wrapped an arm around his wife's shoulder. "It'll be okay, darling."

She nodded, but still looked uncertain.

Then, to my alarm, her eyes shot toward where I stood on the beach. She was looking so directly at me that for a moment I feared that perhaps the invisibility spell Amaya had placed on me had worn off. But looking down, I couldn't see my feet, and since I was making contact with the mermaid, her body was also invisible.

My aunt's gaze lingered for a few more moments before she returned her gaze to her brother.

"What's wrong?" Derek asked.

She shook her head. "It's nothing, Derek. You, Sofia and the rest… You do what you have to do. I think this pregnancy is just making me extra sensitive to… things."

My aunt, I knew, had a gift of sight.

I had to be careful of her.

As they exchanged words of affection and bade their goodbyes, I couldn't ignore the slight tugging deep inside of me. It felt like these people were missing pieces from my life.

And yet overshadowing everything was a burning

feeling of resentment. Of frustration. Of anger.

Nuriya had revealed to me the way my father had always been treated by them. How my grandfather had gone out of his way to pit him against Derek, how his siblings had always held a bias against him—almost as though he was an outsider—and how neglected he had been by the whole lot of them.

They'd never bothered to take the time to understand why he behaved the way he did. Not his own father, and not even Vivienne—who'd certainly been more partial to him than Derek. Why would they, when it was so easy to just label him as the black sheep?

These people were the reason I'd never had the chance to meet my father. The reason I would never meet him.

And they were the reason why Benjamin Novak was prince of this place instead of me.

As Gregor Novak's eldest son, my father should've been ruling over this magnificent island today. Even when my father had still been living, Derek Novak had taken the spotlight—for no reason other than some so-called prophecy that he was to be the one to lead.

Indignation boiled up within me, as it always did whenever I thought of the injustices done to my father. I breathed in deeply, regaining control of my temper and calming my mind.

As the dragons shifted into their beastly state and the crowd of vampires climbed onto their backs, I forced myself to think of more positive things—like how perfectly The Shade's rulers leaving along with all these dragons had panned out for me. I couldn't have asked for better timing.

I remained in my spot, watching as the dragons disappeared into the overcast sky, before continuing on my way. I sped up into a sprint, moving away from the beach, through the woods, until I reached the most rural and least inhabited part of the island. I stopped at the end of a sprawling field where an abundance of vegetables were growing.

I set my eyes on a small wooden building at the far end of it. I guessed that it had once been the house of a farmer, or perhaps a family of fieldworkers. From the state Amaya and I had found it in, it clearly hadn't been stepped inside for years. Which made it the perfect temporary residence for the witch and me. She had fixed a few leaky holes and made it overall more comfortable, and this had been our shelter since arriving in The Shade.

I traveled the rest of the way to our residence, and, gripping the old handle, pushed the door open and stepped inside.

I was pleased to see that Amaya had not gone wandering anywhere. She was sitting on a wooden rocking chair and looked up the moment I entered.

Sensing that it was me, she removed the invisibility spell, her eyes widening as I lowered the body of the mermaid down onto the wooden floorboards.

"I wasn't expecting you back so soon," she said, moving closer toward the mermaid.

"I wasn't expecting it either."

She crouched down and gripped the hair of the mermaid, tugging roughly at it as she examined the state of her.

"You know what to do now," I said.

She looked up, locking eyes with me. She nodded, a stoic expression on her face.

"I'll start preparing the potion," she replied.

Amaya lit the old stove and placed on top of it a black cauldron that she had managed to swipe from Corrine's spell room—along with an assortment of other ingredients. As the witch picked up a rusted blade and stooped down to slice off the first sliver of flesh from the mermaid's tail, I stepped back out of the cabin.

I moved away from the building—and the creature's groaning—and further into the fields. I stopped once I reached their borders. I breathed in the rich woody scent emitting from the soil, still moist from the light rain we'd had earlier in the day. A refreshing breeze blew against my skin. I listened to the humming of the birds, and the whispering of the trees.

As I stood there, relishing the peace and beauty of the island, even in the midst of adversaries, I felt closer to what I imagined home should feel like than I ever had in my life.

And although his time here was long past, I also felt closer to my father. Closer than I'd ever hoped to feel. And soon, I would feel closer still.

Once my ode to him was complete.

READY FOR THE NEXT PART OF BEN & RIVER'S STORY?

A Shade of Vampire 20: A Hero of Realms
is available to order now from Amazon!.
It releases November 18th 2015.

Please visit www.bellaforrest.net for details!

Also, I had mentioned at the back of *A Trail of Echoes* that *A Hero of Realms* would be the final book in Ben's series. I'd fully intended it to be so, however as the time came for writing *A Hero of Realms,* I realized due to the scope and epicness of what's to come, it just wasn't possible for me to do justice to the story in one last book.

This coupled with the fact that I've been swamped with reader emails complaining about Ben's series being so short, made me decide that *A Hero of Realms* will **not** be the last book in Ben's series.

As always, I'm super excited to continue this journey,

and I'm thrilled to have you alongside me for the ride.

Thank you for reading.

Love,

Bella x

P.S. I hope you like the cover on the next page for A Hero of Realms!

P.P.S. If you'd like to stay up to date about my new releases, please visit: www.forrestbooks.com, enter your email and you'll be the first to know.

a hero of

realms

A Shade of Vampire, Book 20

BELLA FORREST

CPSIA information can be obtained at www.ICGtesting.com
Printed in the USA
LVOW11s2144230916

505968LV00002B/60/P

9 781517 417628